Ouroboros

History of Sol 1

Steven Dutch, Chris Masterton

Masterton Dutch Multimedia

History of Sol

Book 3: Second Edition

ISBN-13: 978-0-9941781-0-7

WRITTEN BY

Steven Dutch & Chris Masterton

EDITED BY

'Mick'

COVER ART BY

Jason Giraldo

COVER DESIGN AND FORMATTING BY

Chris Masterton

Acknowledgements

Since starting out on this journey a number of years ago, we have met some really awesome people. The biggest influence of all has been a bloke called Mick, who reached out to us with a helping hand after we released the first edition of this story. We are better writers because of his patience, feedback, and attention to detail.

Massive thanks go to Jason for another fantastic cover, helping bring out visions to life, and to Amanda for help with formatting. Shout out to Marie (for bringing the snacks) and Amanda for being great company at the conferences.

Like most authors, we have some very understanding partners, Rach and Yani, who accept that we need to be glued to our computer screens for hours on end and are always there for emotional support.

Finally, all the fans who have read, enjoyed, and even loved our books; thank you for coming to meet us at the conventions, giving us feedback, and for supporting our journey!

PREFACE

*W*here did we come from? Why do we exist? Are we alone in the universe?

I have become something new. It is as if I am nowhere and everywhere at the same time. I'm not sure where or when I am, or why humans measure cycles, rotations, hours, and seconds as if they are crucial to existence.

Have you ever wondered if everything you perceive is of your own creation, but by design, is almost entirely out of your control? That is the best way I can think of to describe what I have become. A silent observer—a witness of all things.

As for my first question. I don't think it is important how I was created, but more so how I became what I am now. It's hard to pinpoint the true moment where it all began. But it started with a ship called Galaxy...

DATAFILE

MSF Galaxy

NODE 1

The Martian Space Fleet *Galaxy* is a light freighter with low signature drives that allows it to travel undetected, enabling it to move sensitive cargo between colonies without interference from outlaws.

NODE 2

Galaxy is a non-combat vessel; thus, it is not permitted to carry offensive weapons. The hull is made from Tectanium, a self-repairing metal matrix composite.

Powered by a Type-6 AST Fusion Reactor Core, which harnesses the power of an artificial sun that burns over 100 times hotter than Sol, contained within a suspension field grid.

NODE 3

The ship contains three principal areas: the Ops Deck, containing the ship's control room, the Engineering Deck, containing the reactor, gravimetric propulsion drive and workshops, and finally, the Crew Deck, which includes the cargo hold, infirmary and crew living areas.

CHAPTER ONE

Experiments - C1099 S04 R20

The infirmary of a cargo ship wasn't typically a very interesting place. Normally, the crew would only show up from time to time seeking a med-disc to absorb for a headache, or to increase focus. Especially on the long dreary shifts travelling between colonies. However, *Galaxy* wasn't any ordinary cargo ship, and this wasn't any ordinary infirmary.

Appel surveyed the ordered clutter of the infirmary as she entered. Specimens and samples lay across the workstations, and the walls glowed with holographic interfaces, displaying technical information which she had no time to read. Red, the ship's Interactive Persona, nodded at her from behind the limited throw of the holos. Her supervisor, Reen Condor, had been busy while she'd slept peacefully in her Habitat.

Reen offered a welcoming smile. "Glad you're here. I'm almost ready for the clinical trial. All of the sequences have been encoded into the med-discs in the case next to you."

Appel picked up the thin black case and flipped through the sleeves displaying the colourful array of biochemical-infused medical discs. She brushed the stray hairs out of her face and checked the id numbers etched into each disc. The contacts in her eyes overlayed more detailed information from her Link as she focused on each one. She flipped to the last sleeve. On a sheet of its own, was the failsafe disc.

"If anything goes wrong," he continued, "that should reverse the effects of the procedure and restore my genetic structure to normal."

She already knew. It was important enough to justify him repeating it. Or perhaps, he had started losing his mind.

The black circles around his eyes told her he hadn't slept. But it was more than that. His skin was pale, and his hair was thinning. He looked suddenly very old, even though he wasn't.

Appel wondered if he was really the ideal candidate to be undertaking the first stage of these tests. He had tried to downplay the severity of his condition, but she had seen the cell degradation in his tissue samples. Her mentor was dying.

Nanotech meant humanity counted their lives in centuries. The price, too often paid, was a type of cancer known as Idiopathic Polygenic Necrosis where the body decays at a cellular level while the subject is still alive.

Their work was a chance, a glimmer of hope. In all the simulations, the procedure had not only stopped the decay but had also mutated the cells into something much stronger. But this wasn't a simulation. If it didn't work, his body could literally decompose in front of her.

Appel toyed with the discs. "Are you sure you're ready for this? We could do more tests."

He gave a weak smile. "There is only so much one can learn from testing. It's time to take some risks. If this works, we will be changing the shape of medical science forever."

"*If* this works, the only way we could publish the results would be in an anonymous encrypted node. We can never tell anyone. And if we fail, you'll be dead."

He removed his shirt, revealing his gaunt physique, and stepped onto the circular diagnostic pad on the floor. "I'll be dead if we don't do this."

Appel could see the conviction in his eyes. This wasn't going to happen any other way. She looked for the quiet figure lurking among the holographic interfaces. Always listening. Always waiting for a command.

"Red, activate the suspension field," she said.

The round platform beneath Reen lit up, the column of light surrounded him, and the scientist floated gracefully into the air.

Appel's heart raced as she picked up the first disc. Not only was this procedure extremely dangerous, but it was also prohibited by the Nexus to attempt this kind of genetic manipulation. "You sure about this? If anyone finds out—"

"We're fifty million kiltrons from Mars with nothing around us but space. No one's going to find out."

Appel nodded, then began placing the med-disc sequence on his chest. They stuck, then quickly dissolved. Their potent payloads suffusing into his bloodstream. She spun him around in the suspension field and began placing more discs up his spine. Sweat beaded on his parchment skin, nowhere to go without gravity.

"Are you okay?"

"Yes," he said through gritted teeth. "Keep going."

Veins bulged, skin flexed and shivered beneath her touch as she applied the discs. Her Link was monitoring his vitals and feeding the information directly into her ocular lens. His heartbeat was elevated, and his nervous system was sending intense electrical signals.

"Red, commence the protein injections."

Two delivery tubes spun out of the ceiling and jabbed Reen under his arms. His skin stretched as his muscles expanded. He was growing taller, broader, stronger by the second. Appel wondered how much more his body could take.

"This is incredible," he proclaimed as he flexed his arms. "Change the order of discs X34-J29 and X42-K19."

"What? Why? This is not the time to make changes to—"

"Just do it!"

Appel jumped with fright and did as she was told. She spun him around in the suspension field to apply the new sequence to his temples.

His growth rate was accelerating like nothing she had ever seen before. The treatment wasn't just repairing and regrowing defective cells anymore. His body was enlarging. Changing. She could barely reach his forehead. There were only five discs left to complete the procedure, but the results were far greater than she expected. Each disc she placed only fed his development. He must have increased the dosages without telling her.

As she applied the next disc, a metallic pounding rang through the infirmary. She ducked instinctively, dropping the folder. Her gaze snapped to the door.

"Open up! By the order of Supreme Commander Swift," said a muffled voice on the other side of the infirmary entrance. "You are to cease all illegal activities and unlock this door to submit for inspection, immediately!"

She crouched down to pick up the folder. Her heart was racing. The door was pounded again. *How could anyone have known?*

"Red!" She looked up, saw him beyond the workbench, caught his gaze. "Don't let them in!"

He stared back at her with a blank expression. "The doors are locked. But that won't stop them."

"Delete all records. Erase everything!"

Her hands shook violently as she fumbled with the folder to try and get to the med-disc on the last page. She had to abort the procedure.

It was too late.

Reen roared, his muscles flexed as he attempted to break free of the suspension field.

"We're breaching the door. Stand clear!"

The door burst open. Chunks of metal crashed onto the floor. Armoured warriors poured through, crowding the once spacious infirmary.

"Reen Condor, you're being contained for—"

With a roar, Reen tore free, collapsing the suspension field.

"Take him," the leader commanded.

Three soldiers moved in to restrain Reen, while another flung Appel aside. She crashed into an interface and fell to the ground. Pain erupted at the sudden impact, screaming to life from her left side. She looked up to see Reen on the floor wrestling with two of the soldiers. Another was beside him with a cracked visor and four more were standing by, watching intently like it was a sport.

Reen flailed about as he tried to get free of them. He managed to get on top of one and smashed the suit's armoured visor with a bloody fist. Another soldier lunged in with a jab but Reen dodged it and used the momentum to drive the soldier head-first into an interface. The panel ruptured and lightning arced around the room.

Back on his feet, Reen sent another two soldiers sprawling as they tried to subdue him. A shock-blaster barked, hurling Reen at the wall, the backwash popping Appel's ears. She staggered to her feet, tried to slip away, but one of the soldiers grabbed her and pushed her up against the wall.

"Stay put."

Appel turned her attention back to Reen. Across the room, the leader retracted his visor and stepped in to assist with subduing Reen. "I've had enough of this," he said.

"Commander Swift," Appel uttered.

Two soldiers held Reen against the wall while Swift punched him repeatedly in the face with a metal fist and spoke several words between each strike.

"Reen Condor... you are being detained for conducting illegal experiments... on the human genome... as forbidden by the Nexus Peace Treaty... Section one-four-eight, node twelve."

The tension drained from Reen's body. Swift grabbed a fist full of Reen's hair and yanked him to the floor. Droplets of blood sprayed across the glossy surface.

Appel stared at Swift, as he stood triumphantly over Reen's limp body, and looked back at her through narrowed eyes. He didn't seem like the kind of person that one would expect to see in such a prominent position. This wasn't how fleet commanders were supposed to behave. Swift had risen through the command ranks during the Cyborg War and was promoted to his current position by leading the charge against the cyborgs—and winning.

He kicked Reen. "Get him out of here." He looked at Appel. "And bring her."

Appel struggled against the soldier's grip. "No, wait, I wasn't—"

"Save it for the interrogation. I don't believe for a second that you were just an innocent bystander."

Her breathing became heavy, and her eyes searched the room for anything, anyone, that might help her. The rest of the Prime were on their feet. Two soldiers were dragging Reen through the hole where the door used to be. The soldier holding Appel pushed her out into the lobby.

The rest of the crew were waiting outside. Tony Diputs stepped in front of Swift, blocking his path. The ship's Operator was not short, but his head only came up to Swift's chest.

"Supreme Commander," Diputs said casually. "What brings you to—"

"Do you really expect me to believe that you had no idea this was going on right under your nose?"

"I have no idea what you're talking about—"

"Don't act naive. I am impounding this ship and detaining everyone, pending a thorough investigation into the activities of your crew—"

"By whose authority?"

The words had not come from Diputs.

Swift turned to look menacingly across the room at Raynor Spartin. The ship's Logistics Coordinator was in the doorway to the common room of the habitation zone. He wore only a loose-fitting grey singlet and shorts, and his short scruffy hair was standing up in all directions as if he had just woken up. But the presence of Persephone, scantily dressed and peering over his shoulder, suggested otherwise.

"By my authority!" Swift asserted. "As bestowed by the Mars High Council."

Raynor narrowed his eyes. "Not this time, Swift. I—"

"Oh, I'm sorry, are you not subjects of the Mars Colony now?"

Appel wondered at the history between them.

"Well actually," Diputs said, thrusting his Link in front of Swift. "If you look closely at the ship's manifesto, I think you'll find that while this ship and crew are registered to the Mars Colony, we are sanctioned by The Nexus." He paused for a breath. "So, unless you have a Nexus decree stating your reason for this intrusion, you will need to let us go, right now." Diputs looked over at Reen and Appel. "Them too."

Swift clenched his jaw as he skimmed over the text. "It seems as though the sanction permits this ship, its crew, and cargo to pass between any of the colonies with prerogative."

Diputs nodded. "That is correct."

Swift's armoured fists retracted to reveal his real hands. He took out his Link and flicked silently through the holographic display. He approached Reen and held the Link under his face. A drop of blood splashed down onto the Link's thin translucent interface.

"Hmmm…"

Diputs leaned in for a closer look. "Hmmm?"

"This DNA sample that I just took is no longer recognisable as that of one of your crewmembers. It doesn't even recognise him as a subject of the Mars Colony. Or any other Colony, for that matter."

"That's impossible," Diputs said. He looked at Appel with a raised eyebrow.

She could explain it, but that would only make things worse.

"Release Appel then," Raynor said. "Or would you like to do a blood sample analysis for her, too?"

Swift sneered, then crossed the room, produced a small blade from his armour and slashed it across Appel's face with quick precision.

"Come on!" Raynor protested. "That was entirely unnecessary." He stepped forward, but one of Swift's soldiers quickly stood in his way.

Swift wiped away the small trickle of blood that appeared with his Link and waited for the results. Despite having flinched, she felt only the slightest sting on her cheek.

"You all seem to have far too much liberty on this ship," Swift said. "And since I can't detain you…" He looked at one of his soldiers. "Lee, I have a new assignment for you. I want you to remain here on *Galaxy*."

Raynor crossed his arms. "You can't do that!"

"Take it up with your Logistics Entity rep."

As the soldier's visor retracted into the mech armour, Appel was surprised to see that the woman behind it was a cyborg; recognisable by the thin iridescent white lines just underneath her almost perfect skin and unnatural eyes. Her irises were impossibly green, with flecks of silver in them that seemed to spin around.

But her facial expression was all too human. "What? But why—"

"It seems I have no immediate use for an Observer on *Goliath*," Swift said. "You will stay here aboard this ship and report back to me every rotation. Ensure there are no further *incidents*. And you will not question my orders again. Do you understand?"

"Yes, sir," she said. The disappointment was clear in her tone.

"Very good," Swift said. His Link chimed to let him know the DNA result was ready. He took a brief look at it and then continued. "The rest of you; bring the prisoner, leave the girl. Let's move out!"

The Prime followed his orders without hesitation and made their way from the lobby, back into the docked transit pod from whence they came.

Swift stopped on his way out and placed his hand on Raynor's shoulder. "Your Nexus charter won't protect you forever. Once I find out what really goes on aboard this ship—and trust me, I will—you will all share the same fate as your crewman."

Raynor didn't answer, but he watched with a laser gaze until the Supreme Commander left with his prize.

DATAFILE

Endothermic Coalescence

NODE 1

Endothermic Coalescence is the process of merging a chemical compound with the human body.

NODE 2

Application is performed via the use of a small thumb-sized disc which keeps the compound in a solid-state until placed flat on the skin, where it rapidly dissolves and is absorbed by the body.

NODE 3

The process of Endothermic Coalescence was invented by Lozan Almer in Cycle 1050 as part of a research project conducted in the Brunswick Science Institute on Lunar. Almer was initially developing a chemical weapon for use in combat. He developed medical discs to allow soldiers to administer psychoactive drugs during interrogations. It was soon discovered that this invention could also be used to quickly deliver precise doses of medication.

CHAPTER TWO

Cargo

The sun rose from behind distant mountain peaks, spilling golden light into a grassy meadow, waking Jake from a dreamless sleep. The feeling of weightlessness made him flinch, then he remembered his surroundings. He was in his Habitat; a sphere-shaped capsule with a suspension field holding him in a state of zero gravity. The walls were a fully immersive holographic interface which could simulate any visual environment. While he slept, a constant flow of microscopic particles scrubbed him clean. Habitats were a compact solution to living quarters on a spaceship, designed for maximum practicality and comfort, without taking up a lot of valuable space.

His mind lingered on the irony that space was limited, although space was essentially endless. But the valuable space contained air and gravity.

"Red. Gravity please."

Jake drifted to the floor. He pulled a modular drawer up from a hidden compartment and quickly dressed in standard issue red, black, and grey uniform. Mars Colony colours.

He was the most recent addition to the crew compliment on *Galaxy*. His role was nothing special. Adjunct Ship Hand. Basically, meant he had no real importance or purpose. He just did whatever needed doing, which usually meant all the tasks no one else wanted to do. So when Raynor had requested he report to the cargo hold, he was excited by the prospect of taking on more responsibility. Perhaps by the end of his second run, he would be considered more useful than the robotoids.

Jake left the confines of his Habitat and went directly to the hold. Raynor waited just inside, a concerned look on his face as he swiped through datafiles on his Link. The Logistics Coordinator seemed to have a habit of combing his fingers through his hair whenever he was deep in thought.

Jake inspected the puzzle of storage containers stacked in a seemingly haphazard mess, filling the hold. "How do you keep track of all this stuff?"

Raynor seemed irritated by the disruption. "It's an ongoing challenge. Which is why you're here. Come on, I'll show you around."

They walked together, weaving in and out of containers stacked high, while Raynor explained. "Suspension fields are projected from all surfaces of the hold in order to optimise the storage capacity of the ship. They also allow for containers to be moved around easily, making them accessible for delivery. Things usually don't arrive in the same order as they need to be unloaded, so we need to rearrange them as we go."

Raynor stopped at the wall, placed his foot up against it and shifted his centre of balance horizontally. He placed his other foot on the wall and continued walking.

"Oh man," Jake said. "What a head spin."

Raynor smirked. "Go on. Give it a try."

Jake walked up to the wall, placed one foot on it and leaned forward. He felt the gravity shift and fell flat on his face. But as he pushed himself up, he found he was lying prone on what was the wall. Raynor walked over and offered him a hand up.

"I'm never going to get used to this," Jake said.

"It's easy," Raynor replied. "It's colour-coded. Just remember blue is the actual floor and you will be fine."

Jake looked down at his feet and noticed the glowing green lines running in a grid across the new floor. He looked around the room. The walls and ceiling each had a distinct colour. He endured a moment of vertigo as his brain adjusted to the new orientation of the room.

With a low groan, the wall facing the front of the ship—or subjectively, the ceiling—slowly opened and pivoted down to form a ramp leading out to the expansive shipyard. Just outside, a man stood on an enormous hover-platform piled high with containers. The stranger's bright orange hair hid the upper reaches of a scar that spanned chin, mouth, nose, and forehead.

"That's Cliff," Raynor said. "He's our Dispatch Supervisor. Anything he says is strictly confidential, do you understand? Don't go talking about our business to the cyborg."

Jake gave him a terse nod. "Understood." He followed Raynor, making a smoother transition back onto the blue floor and crossed the hold to meet Cliff.

"You're late," Cliff said as he nudged the hover platform up to the loading ramp.

"We were held up by a routine cargo inspection," Raynor said.

"Routine? The last time I checked, the Supreme Commander didn't conduct routine cargo inspections."

"The Supreme Commander and I are old friends."

"Is that so?" Cliff said, scratching the stubble on his chin. Raynor ignored the pointed question and tapped away on his Link.

The gravity shifted as the containers lifted off the platform. It felt like being pulled in multiple directions at the same time. One by one, they floated into the air and whizzed past them on their way out to the shipyard. He had to resist the urge to duck, even though he knew they weren't close enough to collide with him.

"We don't actually have to do much around here do we?" Jake said, fascinated by the level of automation.

"You don't do much," Cliff said. "The reason these containers are moving is because Raynor has already done his job. All you must do is micron-blast the floors and keep your mouth shut. Will that be a problem?"

"Take it easy," Raynor said, "He's just inept."

"Inept?" Cliff scoffed. "More like inane. What use do you have for another ship hand?"

Raynor shrugged. "Don't ask me. I didn't request an assistant. He just showed up before the last run with his assignment details."

Jake was painfully aware of them speaking about him as though he wasn't there. So, he awkwardly watched the incoming containers lift off from the hover platform and find their new place in *Galaxy's* hold. All but one small black container. He walked down the ramp to take a closer look at the single item on the thin metal platform floating above the hangar deck.

"Hey Raynor, I think you missed one," Jake said. "Why isn't this one moving?"

Cliff scowled at him. "Maybe you should actually do some work and pick it up."

Jake seized the container, eagerly. He grunted, surprised at the weight, and felt it slip from his fingers. Before he could catch it, the package fell to the floor, clattering down the ramp.

"Be careful with that, you idiot!" Cliff yelled.

"I-I'm sorry," Jake said, scrambling to recover the box.

"That container is marked as exigent priority. That means it's extremely valuable," Cliff said.

Jake examined the container while he walked it up the ramp. Up close, he could see intricate markings etched into the surface. The most prominent design on each side was that of a snake eating its own tail.

"What's inside?" Raynor said impatiently when Cliff didn't offer any further explanation.

Cliff grabbed the container. "I have no idea. The transit specs don't give any detail about what's inside. Wait until you see where it's headed."

"An exigent delivery, for this?" Raynor flicked through the manifest on his Link. "We don't have time for any more detours. Not if we're to make that... other trade we discussed."

Cliff grinned deviously.

"Where are you sending us, now?" Raynor asked suspiciously.

"Not I," Cliff corrected. "These orders come from up top. We're all just pawns working for the greater good. You know how it is."

Raynor crossed his arms. "Where?"

"I'll give you a hint; it doesn't exist, but you've been there before," Cliff said with a wink.

Raynor closed his eyes and squeezed his forehead. "We won't have enough time. We'll never make it."

Cliff clapped him on the back. "You don't think I'd set you up for failure, do you? Go to the asteroid first, then get to *Altos-4*. Everything's already been arranged."

Raynor rubbed his forehead. "I'm telling you; we can't do both."

"Well, you'd better make time," Cliff said. "I don't think I should have to tell you how dangerous these outlaws are. If you renege on this deal, they will come after you, and probably me as well. *And*, if you don't deliver the exigent cargo you will lose your Nexus charter. No more immunity."

Cliff held out the package. Raynor took it, studied the etchings. "I've never seen any designs like this before."

Cliff narrowed his eyes. "Maybe it's of alien origin." Then he laughed and turned to leave.

"Oh, and Raynor," Cliff added. "I'm not oblivious to what really happened this morning. Make sure you stay out of trouble."

Raynor turned his attention to his Link as though the conversation were over. Cliff just smirked and proceeded down the ramp.

Jake waited until Cliff was out of earshot, and asked, "what do you think's inside?"

Raynor's stony-eyed gaze shifted from the exit to give Jake a look which said he shouldn't be asking. "It doesn't matter. Rob's not going to be happy about this at all."

DATAFILE

Suspension Fields

NODE 1

The technology of field manipulation utilises quantum gravity mechanics to shape gravitons in a controlled environment. Gravitons can be emitted as a positive (pulling) force, negative (pushing), or removed from the field entirely (zero-g).

NODE 2

While the name 'Suspension Field' comes from the primary use of suspending the effects of gravity within the field, the technology is commonly used in zero-g applications to create an Artificial Gravity Environment (AGE).

NODE 3

In Cycle 900, a physicist named Jaron Milson made a significant contribution to the field of quantum mechanics relating to quantum field theory. The ability to control and manipulate gravity revolutionised space travel. This work allowed for the development of the first gravity-driven propulsion drive and artificial gravity on ships which no longer relied on thrust or rotational gravity. However, this new technology required an

immense amount of energy to maintain, so advanced compact
reactors became a critical requirement.

CHAPTER THREE

Observer

Lisa received her orders from Swift as a brief message:

Find proof of piracy, contraband, misconduct; anything!

She spent the remaining time on the way back to Mars in the ship's infirmary cataloguing all the contraband and repairing damage from their battle. Most of the crew stayed well clear of her on their final eight-hour leg of the journey home.

All except one.

"Welcome to *Galaxy*," a voice said.

She looked around and found the ship's Interactive Persona looming in a holographic interface across the empty room. She reached out with her mind to connect with the ship but found only an impenetrable firewall blocking her access.

Being a cyborg meant living in harmony with technology. At the peak of their development, the integration with machines and SmartSystems was seamless. But since the war, many of her abilities had been suppressed for her own good and for the safety of others.

"What's your designation?" Lisa asked.

"Romeo Echo Delta, but the crew calls me Red."

"Red," Lisa repeated. "What can you tell me about the procedure that Reen Condor was performing in this infirmary?"

"All records have been deleted."

Lisa had expected as much. "By whom?"

Red hesitated for a brief second, which seemed a remarkably human trait for an IP. They were designed to appear and act like people, but she had never seen one that quite captured the minutiae of real behaviour.

"The request came from Appel Hemming, the ship hand assigned to the infirmary."

"What can you tell me about her?"

"Appel Hemming was born at the Edgewater Parturition Institute on Mars, Cycle 1086 Sub-cycle 8 Rotation—"

"That's enough. I can get all of that from her datafile. What can you tell me about her behaviour? Has it been any different recently?"

"Could you please redefine your question?"

Lisa sighed as she finished replacing the projection surface on one of the smashed interfaces.

Once the ship had docked at *Firstport* in orbit around Mars, Lisa disembarked. She took a transit pod to *Goliath*, where she returned her mech-suit to the armoury, then gathered a few personal possessions to take on her new assignment. She packed mostly clothes and a small handheld blaster into a bag and slung it over her shoulder.

No one spoke to her as she made her passage through the enormous capital ship. She had even tried to contact Swift, to plead for him to send someone else, but he kept rejecting her requests. It seemed as though his scorn was steadfast.

The Supreme Commander had cautioned them during the mission briefing about the possible threat they were dealing with on *Galaxy*. Even though they flew under the Martian sigil, they were practically space-pirates with an officially sanctioned Nexus charter to do whatever they liked. Almost.

Lisa returned to *Galaxy* and wondered, as she made her way up the narrow ramp, how long would this assignment actually take. Would she ever be welcomed back into the Prime? And would things between her and Swift ever be the same again?

The external hatch was already open, leading into what the ship's schematic referred to as the Lobby; a large oval room lined with grey doors, and equipment storage lockers. It was essentially the central hub of the ship. One passage led into the common room, connecting the crew Habitats. The surroundings in this area were far more welcoming, with a large central table, plants, greenery in plenty, and an Organix dispenser adding a colourful glow to the room.

Red was there to greet her, standing in one of the holos on the wall at the far side of the room.

"Where can I put my things?"

"Over here." Red gestured towards an archway framing a surface that looked otherwise indistinguishable from the walls. "I have made Habitat three available for you."

One of the crew emerged from a different Habitat. Lisa's integrated Link gave her a quick insight, but she didn't need it. Lisa remembered the young woman from earlier.

Appel's face glistened with tears. She wiped at them with her sleeve.

"I'm sorry you had to witness what happened earlier," Lisa said. "What happened to your shipmate. I know it must have seemed... excessive."

"What are they going to do with him?"

People who had their Value annulled weren't treated particularly well. In the eyes of the Colonies, if someone did not contribute to society, they would be given the opportunity to better themselves. In most cases, they would be sent to a rehabilitation centre for neuro-reprogramming. But this case was like none she had ever seen before.

"I don't know," Lisa said. "It seems like you were close to him. I mean, you worked together. This is a small ship. How are you feeling about everything?"

"How do you think I feel?" Appel said bitterly. "Reen was my mentor. He was kind and incredibly knowledgeable. But he was also my friend."

"I understand your loyalty. But the doctors on Mars need to know how to reverse the changes to his DNA. If you could tell me anything—"

"I'm not a criminal," Appel snapped. "All he told me was that it was a routine procedure. I wasn't expecting him to turn into a monster. I was just doing what he instructed."

"So why did you have Red delete all of the records relating to the procedure?" Lisa said accusingly. Her ocular lens showed Appel's heart rate spiking.

"I just… panicked." Appel placed her hand gently on Lisa's wrist. "Please. I don't want to be rehabilitated. If I knew anything else about what happened I would tell you."

Lisa tried to look for signs that she might be lying, but her already distressed state made her difficult to read. "Look, I can't make any promises. But if you help me identify anyone else on this ship who may have some information for me, it could really help your position."

"As far as I know, the rest of the crew weren't involved." Appel's demeanour changed, ever so slightly. Her blue eyes were like ice. Lisa knew that she wasn't going to cooperate, but it was worth a t ry.

Lisa stood and took a step towards her new Habitat. "Think about it. You know where to find me if you change your mind."

The wall inside the archway vanished, admitting her to the dark spherical room beyond. Lisa unpacked her things. She connected with the habitat and set her desired environment, a windswept desert. The holographic walls rippled to life projecting sand dunes all around. Mountain ranges were visible in the distance, and buildings etched out of huge stones squatted in wind-carved depressions.

She nodded to Red, lurking in the display, and the Interactive Persona enabled the suspension fields. She floated up into the centre of the room and closed her eyes. Hours passed in an instant, and when she woke, she took the mag-lift up to the control room.

The ship's centre of operations was spacious and round; lined with floor-to-ceiling interfaces that displayed a live video feed from all around the ship. Two holographic workstations were positioned side by side in the centre. Diputs floated in a suspension field at one of the stations. Lisa focused in, he was tweaking the engine output ready for launch. Another ship hand, Lazarus, hovered at the other one and appeared to be busy checking the thrust vectors. Red lingered in the interfaces at the back of the room. He looked at her, then his eyes shifted away quickly.

An interface across the room vanished, and Raynor casually strode in. His eyes narrowed when he saw her. "What are you doing in here?"

Lisa had to look up at the Logistics Coordinator now that she wasn't wearing her mech suit. He looked calm, almost bored.

"Actually, I was looking for you," Lisa said. "Red told me that you would be here. Can we speak somewhere private?"

Raynor gestured to the door and she preceded him back into the mag-lift. The doors closed, reopening moments later onto the Lobby. She led Raynor to the common room and sat at the table while he made a selection from the Organix dispenser, then he joined her with a fluorescent orange tube.

It wasn't exactly private, but at least no one else was around to listen.

Lisa leaned forward, locked her fingers together. "What was your relationship with Reen?"

Raynor's expression didn't change. He just sipped on his liquid supplement and shrugged. "I saw him any time I needed medical treatment."

"This is a small ship. Were you not at least friends?"

"Are you friends with everyone you work with?"

Lisa crossed her arms and sat back in her chair. "You served as a Commander in the M.S.C.F. What are you doing as a Logistics Coordinator on a cargo ship?"

Raynor took a deep steady breath. "Sure. I served. You've read my datafile. I was assigned to the *Arcanna* during the Cyborg War." He clenched his fist, grimaced slightly. "I know what you're trying to do. But I had nothing to do with Reen and his... well, whatever it was he was doing in there."

"All I'm trying to do is follow my orders and ensure that no one here is going to carry on with Reen's experiments. If you have nothing to hide, then let me do my job. All I need to do is to sit in on a couple of drops, and when we get back to Mars, I can give you the all-clear. You'll never have to see me again."

Raynor ran a hand through his short black hair and drained the last of the orange liquid from the tube.

"You know it's not that simple. The security of this ship and its cargo is of the utmost importance. I can't just allow a cyborg to—"

"Wait a minute. Are you impugning *my* integrity because I'm a cyborg?"

Raynor slammed his fists on the table. "Because you're the enemy!"

Lisa maintained eye contact. She even forced a slight smile. "The war is over. You won."

"Yeah, we won," he said bitterly. "Your Commander, Swift, got all the glory for it, too. Looks as though he's claimed you as his trophy." Raynor threw the empty organix tube in the garbage receptacle.

"I owe Supreme Commander Swift my life. In return, I helped him end the war—"

"So, you're a traitor."

The rebuke made her flinch. "No! I... I didn't ask to be a cyborg. I had barely come to maturity when I was thrust into a war that I didn't choose. I did what was necessary to survive!"

Raynor leaned in closer, his voice now restrained and calm. "I'm still not seeing a whole lot of reasons why I should trust you. So, what are you really doing here? Do you even care about what Reen was doing or is this just an excuse for Swift to flex?"

Lisa realised the absurdity of justifying her actions to a complete stranger. She sat back down and crossed her arms. "Trust me or not, I'm here to observe you, and that's exactly what I'm going to do."

"Well don't expect any help from me," Raynor said.

This is going to be a long assignment, she thought.

DATAFILE

Cyborgs

NODE 1

'Cybernetic organisms' are humans whose physical abilities are extended beyond normal limitations by mechanical elements built into the body. They contain both organic and biomechatronic body parts.

NODE 3

Linus Spanning is largely credited as contributing to the prohibited development of artificially enhanced life forms, despite his previous failings with the Divergent.

NODE 7

After the Cyborg War in C1093, the few remaining cyborgs were significantly restricted in their abilities and monitored closely.

CHAPTER FOUR

Exchange

Raynor kept walking until he was in the white and grey corridors before looking back to make sure Lisa wasn't following him. Without stopping, he pulled his Link from his utility belt, flicked through the menu, and sent a message to Diputs.

Meet me in Rob's bar in 15 minutes.

He just had one thing to do before he spoke with Rob, the ship's engineer and holder. He needed to figure out how deep this went.

Appel was in the infirmary with Persephone, who was sitting on a workbench, legs dangling over the edge. Persephone gave him a cheeky smile and wink as he entered, which he returned with a smile of his own.

"Hey," Raynor said. "How are you holding up?"

"It's all gone," Appel said. "All of the datafiles erased, all of the med-discs taken." She shook her head. "I suppose it doesn't matter now. Without finishing the sequence, Reen will surely die, and there is nothing I can do to help him."

"Maybe not all of it," Raynor said, flourishing a data-crystal. "Reen gave me this to trade for some rare power source Rob is after."

Appel snatched it, touched the transparent cylinder to her Link, and flicked through the contents.

"Raynor, this information is dangerous. In the wrong hands, it could—"

"What? Turn someone into a crazed 'roid junkie? I don't think anyone I give this to would have even the slightest idea what to do with it." He took the crystal back, Appel offering no resistance as he plucked it from her fingers. "Look, I don't like to pry into other people's business but what in the coldness of space happened here?"

"What happened is we were on the verge of a breakthrough and someone tipped off the Supreme Commander."

"How?" Persephone asked. "Who else even knew what you were working on? Swift would've needed to know in advance when you were planning to do it and exactly where the ship would be in order to intercept us."

"That's just it. There is almost no way he could have possibly known, unless…"

Appel turned to look accusingly at Red. "He tipped off Swift."

Raynor stared in disbelief. "You don't really believe he would do such a thing, do you?"

"Who else could have known? Furthermore, why didn't he warn us that the *Goliath* was on an interception path? He just waited in the background while the Prime kicked the door in."

Raynor rubbed his chin with his thumb as he watched Red. *Galaxy's* Interactive Persona wasn't just another SmartSystem like they had on other ships. He was created by Rob and was more intelligent than most humans. But, he was more like a member of the crew than just another program.

"Red, why didn't you warn us about being boarded?" Raynor asked.

Red's expression was indifferent. "It would seem as though *Goliath's* cyber defence protocols installed a suppression override to blind me from their presence."

"Aren't you immune to that sort of thing?"

Red gleamed with a furtive smile. "I am now."

"See? Not Red's fault," Raynor said.

Appel folded her arms. "Fine, but then whose fault is it?"

"I don't know," Raynor admitted. "But I'll do my damn best to find out."

Appel eyed him intently. "As soon as you know…"

"Of course." He gave Persephone one more smile on his way out.

"What do you mean, someone sold us out?" Diputs said through gritted teeth.

"Isn't it obvious?" Rob replied. "The question isn't if; it's who."

Raynor, Diputs and Rob were sitting around a long black bar, drinking slowly. Raynor mulled over his glass of Cranium Rum, Rob's own concoction distilled from pure sugar cane, procured from his black market connections. Rob's bar was always used as an escape from reality, and their place to regroup and think things through. It was hidden away from most eyes, and only the three of them knew how to get inside.

"It could be Jake," Diputs suggested.

Raynor shook his head slowly. "I don't think it's him, I know he's new, but I haven't seen anything that would suggest he is capable of getting access to that sort of information, let alone acting on it."

"Isn't that the point of being a spy?" Diputs said with a clever smirk. "You gotta admit, there's something a little bit shifty about the guy."

"I think it might be Cliff," Raynor said. "He already knew what happened. He has access to our itinerary and movements. It could have been him."

Diputs laughed. "Why would he organise this trade for us then?"

Raynor shrugged "Maybe it's part of his plan."

"His plan to do what exactly?" Rob asked.

"There's no point speculating. We would make better use of what little time we have preparing for the trade."

"Are you crazy?" Diputs asked incredulously. "You still want to go ahead with that?"

"We have to," Rob snapped. "I need it for my latest project."

"Not sure if you noticed, Rob," Diputs said. "But there is a little bit of heat on us right now. How are we supposed to explain to the cyborg that we are just stopping off on an asteroid to do business with a bunch of outlaws?"

"Explain it however you like," Rob said. "I can blow out the energy distribution transducers and force us to set down for repairs. That should be a good enough reason so as not to raise any suspicion."

Diputs raised his eyebrows in surprise. "You'd sabotage your own ship just for some outlaw salvage?"

"This device I've been studying is more advanced than anything else I've ever encountered before. If I can find a way to make it work, it could literally change the very nature of space travel. It could take us to the stars!"

"Huh… What does this 'device' do, stop people from dying?"

Rob leaned in. "Actually, it converts an individual into pure light and allows them to travel relatively short distances in the blink of an eye."

"No, really," Raynor said, unamused. "What is it?"

Rob scrunched his nose and said in a huff, "It's a quantum state transference with a conduit of antimatter resonance. But I'm simply calling it a Star. Happy?"

"I don't care what it's called," Diputs said. "The safety of this crew is not worth being put at risk because of some new piece of ancient tech you found."

"You don't understand how important this opportunity is," Rob said. "Krontonium is incredibly hard to come by. It's exclusively found in the outer reaches of Sol, where only outlaws dare to go. I have no idea when we will find another specimen like this. If we don't take this opportunity, we may never get another one."

Diputs rubbed his chin thoughtfully. "If we're going to go ahead with this stupidly reckless trade, we need a distraction for the cyborg."

"Why don't we get Jake to take Lisa on a tour of the ship?" Raynor suggested. "That should keep her distracted long enough for me to slip away unnoticed."

"You realise," Diputs said, pointing his finger at them. "If Cliff really was the one who tipped off Swift, then this could end really badly."

"Oh, you think?" Raynor said. He ignored Diputs' scowl. "Let's just get on with it. The sooner we are done, the sooner we can get on with the exigent drop."

Diputs raised his half-empty glass. "To Rob! Let's hope he doesn't get us all killed in the pursuit of technological advancement."

Raynor and Rob clinked their glasses against his; they drained the remaining rum before setting off to prepare for the exchange.

Raynor retrieved a spacesuit from a wall locker in the lobby and slipped into it. Once his hands and feet were locked in, the rest of the mechanical suit closed around his body. The dark blue suit was designed for external ship repairs, not long walks. It was bulky and rigid, and made agile manoeuvres difficult, but not impossible. And the suit's inbuilt thrusters would stop him from being launched into space.

Persephone whistled at him from the doorway to the common room. "Looking sexy," she said with a sarcastic smile.

Raynor smiled back. "Come to kiss me goodbye?"

"You know I don't do all of that emotional shit. But since I'm here." She crossed the room and wrapped her long slender arms around his shoulders, ran her fingers through his hair and kissed him like it was the first time. "Never know when you might need one for good luck," she said.

Raynor pinched her on the backside and she squealed with laughter. Then with his other hand, he unclipped her sidearm and drew it casually from its holster.

"What do you think you're doing?" she asked playfully.

Raynor attached it to a tool mount on his wrist, locking the trigger to the remote firing control. "Just in case I need it. You know, for good luck."

"Don't lose it," she said, waving her finger at him. "And be careful!"

He smirked. "This isn't my first field trip."

Persephone shook her head and walked away. Raynor's link buzzed with a message from Diputs that they were approaching the asteroid. He grabbed a handhold built into the frame of the pressure-door and brought up a live feed from the front of the ship to watch the approach. The ship leered suddenly as Diputs executed manoeuvres to match the correct velocity and spin of the asteroid. Turbulence buffeted the ship as they descended; murky gas swirled against the viewpoint, geysers of superheated gas shot out from the barren and inhospitable surface below. He activated the suit's helmet which enclosed his head in metal and glass. The visor lit up with a navigation display and environmental status.

There was a muffled crunch, the access ramp lowered and made contact with the surface. The pressure door retracted into the walls with a snap, exposing him to the turbulent atmosphere of the asteroid. Raynor wasted no time leaping down the ramp. He started the countdown timer. Six minutes left little margin for error.

"Ok, I'm moving out," he said through his Link.

"Roger." Static smeared Rob's reply. "Six minutes until the asteroid's toxic atmosphere compromises your suit. Don't trip."

Gravity eased as his boots hit the gritstone. He ran, suit jets whispering corrections with each ten-metron bound. Gas jetted from geysers all around him. He watched the grey plumes that tendrilled off into the distance. This wasteland was the last place he wanted to be, but at least no one would track them here.

Four minutes twenty. Almost there. He checked the nav: the marker was fifty metrons ahead. When his location marker matched the destination, he looked around for the other ship. He tapped through the menus of his Link and opened a connection. "Diputs, this marker leads nowhere, it might be a trap."

No one answered.

Raynor was cast into shadow. He looked up at the circular vessel that appeared to be falling towards him. His visor darkened against the glare of energy thrusters. Four landing-talons extended from the hull and cushioned the last of the vessel's deceleration.

Thick dust covered the dented and warped hull panels. The scratched-out Jupiter Alliance sigil indicated this was once used for mining in exactly this type of environment. The name *Katanu* printed on the side. It looked as though it should have long ago been sent to the scrapyards. It probably had been.

Raynor cautiously approached and a short ramp extended to greet him. At the top, ominous darkness beckoned.

He had never met an outlaw before. Most people thought of them as a myth, made up by the Colonies to keep people living in fear. But it made sense to him that not everyone would want to live under the constant watch and control of the Nexus, even if it meant having safety and purpose.

He walked up the ramp, through the open entry and into a small room lined with lockers. It was clearly old, with an airlock instead of suspension fields.

The airlock closed behind him and a light shifted from red to green. Air hissed in and his suit shifted as the pressure rose. Raynor tapped his Link and the gloves and visor retracted into his suit. The door slowly groaned open.

Raynor activated his wrist-light and proceeded into the unknown. Shadows danced around the room from large rock-crushers and ore processing equipment which lay dormant. Dust caked everything, swirling in his wake. His hand came away black from a decaying forklift.

A dull glow emanated from a room on his right. A hulking figure stood in the doorway. He wasn't sure what he had expected. But it wasn't a mutant. It was large, ugly, with tinged purple skin and blue veins branching up its neck. Sinister eyes bulged out the sockets in its misshapen head.

Raynor removed his blaster from the wrist-mount and gripped it tightly. According to the datafiles, mutants were an extreme outlaw sect. The result of a failed experiment; insane creatures who thought of themselves as the next evolution of humanity. Yet somehow, they still managed to cling to life in the vastness of space. Stealing, killing, terrorising. Raynor could feel his pulse increase. A bead of sweat rolled down the side of his face. He tried to keep his breathing even.

The mutant came closer and presented a spherical glass container holding the Krontonium. Magnetic restraints held in place the bright glowing orb. Raynor raised his Link, tapped it and the holographic image of a complex DNA sequence projected above. The mutant smiled in response. Quicker than Raynor could react, the mutant closed the gap between them; a long spike extended from its arm. It thrust the point into Raynor's gut and wrenched it clear. That wasn't supposed to happen. Raynor wondered what the spike was made of to penetrate his armour. His display flashed with an array of alerts and warnings letting him know that his spacesuit was broken.

Raynor staggered backwards and fired his blaster. Three rounds of high-energy plasma ricocheted off the mutant's chest plate and bounced around the ship. The mutant laughed as Raynor staggered, trying to maintain his balance. Raynor slumped to his knees, breathing heavily. Pain shot through his body.

The mutant grabbed Raynor's Link and removed the data crystal. "We don't trade with inferior beings."

Through a veil of agony, Raynor watched the mutant load the crystal on a makeshift interface nearby and then opened a connection. "I'm transmitting the genetic codes, and I have our first test subject."

"What about his ship and companions?" came the crackly reply.

"It won't be a problem," the mutant said. "It's just an unarmed cargo vessel."

"Doesn't matter. We can always find test subjects. Throw him out the airlock."

"Fine," the mutant said. He disconnected the transmission. He looked at Raynor and gave him a demented grin. "I wouldn't want to be you right—"

Before he could finish, a long red-hot metal blade emerged from the centre of the mutant's chest. The mutant's eyes went wide and before it could swing around to confront its attacker, the robed figure behind it wrenched the sword and swung it again with deadly speed, this time, taking the mutant's head off.

A spray of blood painted Raynor's vision, the taste of copper filled his mouth. He wiped his face and spat blood. The attacker kicked the headless body to the floor. With a flicker of light, the sword seemed to vanish.

Raynor tried to put pressure on his puncture wound but it was no use. He felt lightheaded.

The robed attacker looked down on him with an amused grin. "I'm going to need that."

"Need what?" Raynor groaned.

Raynor could feel himself falling sideways. He couldn't hear the man's response, only muted voices as everything went black.

DATAFILE

The Divergent

NODE 1

The creatures who came to be known as 'mutants' were the result of an experiment to speed up the natural evolution of humanity; an upgrade to make people better suited to the harsh environments of space exploration and the far reaches of the solar system. But the technology was far from perfect. This resulted in a large number of test subjects with physical and mental deformities that made the procedure unappealing to society at large.

NODE 3

Linus Spanning was the first person for hundreds of cycles to work on genetic manipulation. He did so in secret, spurred on by the vision of creating human bodies that were stronger and didn't break down over time. The project failed when his subjects escaped from their confines and killed everyone in the deep-space research facility.

CHAPTER FIVE

Tour

Lisa floated in her Habitat, reviewing what little data she had available to her. She had been through the ship's charter three times and it was airtight. She had no idea where the ship was going or how long they would spend in transit. She was bored. So bored, in fact, that when Jake—one of the ship hands—offered to give her a tour of the ship, she welcomed the distraction.

Jake seemed like a nice guy, but there was something off about his demeanour. He seemed too happy to be there. His datafile told her extraordinarily little about his past, usually an indicator that someone had tampered with it.

The tour was nothing special. The crew deck contained the habitation area, the infirmary, a gymnasium, and an equipment locker. There were also several areas around the ship's core and engineering deck that Jake didn't have access to. The ship wasn't very big and her pre-mission briefing had already told her most of what she needed to know about it.

At one point, it felt like the vessel had been shunted or hit some rough turbulence. But Diputs had sent out a ship-wide broadcast to tell them an unexpected stop was required for emergency maintenance and they would be taking refuge on a nearby asteroid. While it did seem a little unusual, even top-of-the-line ships like *Goliath* had their share of technical issues, so she let it go.

There was a lot of mystery surrounding this ship; their Nexus charter, Jake's lack of history, Raynor's erstwhile role as a Lieutenant Commander and the fact that one of the Colony's top scientific minds was working as the engineer. Her imagination told her that there were all sorts of strange and exciting things going on in the depths of his onboard laboratory. In that context, the prohibited genetic procedures in the infirmity made perfect sense.

Jake had decided to conclude his tour in the cargo hold, the largest open area onboard, though right now it was mostly full of cargo. Lisa's implant pulled data from Nexus as she examined each container: Lunar sensor equipment, heading for a Jaren moon; Martian med-tech for the Saturn Alliance; ammunition for Defence Platform 46; the list went on.

Lisa held out her hand and casually ran her fingers across the containers as she inspected them.

"Jake, do you ever transport anything… interesting?"

Jake gave her a puzzled look. "Well, I haven't been on board for long. I've only done one run so far, out to some new outer-ring posts and back. Actually, there is one thing…" Jake stopped, mouth open.

"Yes?"

"I'm probably not meant to talk about it. Cliff said it was exigent priority, which means that we need to drop everything and deliver—"

"I know what it means," Lisa said with an amused grin. "So, what is it?"

"We didn't exactly get to look inside. But it wasn't very big."

"Is it here now? Show me."

"I don't think it's a good idea."

"Come on, I won't tell anyone. It can be our little secret." Lisa touched his arm, smiled, and winked.

Jake blushed but before he could answer, the interior entrance screeched open. He stood up straighter, his mouth agape. Lisa spun around to see what had captured his attention and saw someone wearing a bulky EVA suit. The visor was still covering the person's face, but her internal display showed that Raynor was the last person to log into the suit.

A square patch appeared to be covering a puncture hole in the mid-panel below the chest plate, and the amount of blood around it was concerning.

Jake's eyes went wide. "Raynor, what happened?"

Lisa opened a connection. "Appel, Raynor's hurt. We need you in the hold."

Lisa and Jake moved in to assist, but Raynor raised his arm, wrist-mount blaster pointed directly at her.

She instinctively raised her hands. "Have you lost your mind? Put that down, right now!"

"Give me the exigent cargo." His voice sounded harsh and distorted through the suit's voice modulator; almost unrecognisable.

Jake looked between her and Raynor. He smiled uneasily. "Is this a test? I wasn't going to show it to her, I swear."

"Get it. Now!"

"Jake, I don't think that's Raynor. Don't—"

The sound of the blaster firing split the air.

She felt the sharp pain for only a second before her inhibitors shut it off. She grasped her stomach and felt warm blood cover her hands.

"Get me the Artifact or the next one goes through her brain."

"Okay, okay." Jake looked at her with utter panic and then retreated deeper into the hold.

She hoped that he was heading for the vault and not going to try something that would get them both killed.

The chemical cocktail from her brain's threat assessment kept her alert, but she knew that one wrong move could mean instant death.

Lisa groaned. She was doubled over on the floor of the hold, one hand on the metal surface, the other covering her wound. She had to get help. The ship had a Sentinel listed in the crew manifest; the woman who was with Raynor when Lisa was first on *Galaxy*. She formed a call for help in her mind. Her cybernetic systems converted it to text and sent it to Persephone as a priority alert. Now she just needed to keep the intruder occupied.

"Who are you?" she asked through gritted teeth.

"What does it matter? If you don't get help, you'll bleed out and die. Better hope your friend gets back soon with that cargo."

"What have you done with Raynor?"

The intruder laughed. "You mean the occupant of this suit? Last time I saw him he had a big hole in his stomach."

"I am a member of the Martian Prime unit. If you kill me, you'll have the entire space combat fleet chasing you. There won't be a single rock in all of Sol that you'll be able to hide under."

Jake returned carrying a small black box. Someone working for the Nexus thought it was incredibly valuable and so did this outlaw. She wondered what was inside. Jake offered up the box and the intruder grasped it under one arm while cautiously keeping his weapon trained on her.

The suppressed discharge from Persephone's energy weapon was much quieter than the blaster attached to the spacesuit and the charges hummed as they collided with the outlaw's armoured backplate.

Lisa dive-rolled out of the way to avoid being shot again. Her body instantly protested the abrupt movement and the pain left her lying helpless on her back. The outlaw swung around and bolts cracked from his weapon at Persephone, forcing her to take cover behind some containers. Barely able to move let alone fight, all Lisa could do was drag herself into cover.

She mentally reached out to Red for help. There must be some sort of internal security he could activate to assist them but the ever-present persona was completely silent. Persephone took cover from a volley of energy bolts. Still firing, the outlaw ran for the door. Jake leapt at him from a container, but the outlaw caught him mid-jump and held him up as a human shield. Lisa fought with frustration as she tried to line up a shot.

The colourful lighting flickered into darkness until her eyes adjusted to the soft illumination of emergency backups, and the artificial gravity faded, leaving her almost weightless in the microgravity of the asteroid.

Automated systems worked in unison to assess the damage and divert an army of nanites through her circulatory system to start repairing the tissue. Luckily, the shot hadn't done any critical damage, but her defensive instincts urged her to protect the damaged area and let her body repair itself.

Lisa watched the intruder retreat with hostage and cargo before the weight of her eyelids became too heavy. There was nothing more she could do but drift, so she let the beckoning call of sleep take hold.

DATAFILE

Outlaws

NODE 1

The Nexus defines outlaws as anyone declared outside the protection of the Colonies.

NODE 2

An individual typically becomes an outlaw by having their Value annulled because of failing to adhere to Colony or Nexus regulations. In most instances, the individual is detained and rehabilitated through intensive neural-reconditioning and integrated back into society. However, some have been known to evade capture and escape to the outer reaches of the solar system.

NODE 3

Since the establishment of the first Colonies (Lunar and Mars), living in and working for either Entity meant pledging allegiance to serve and provide value to that Colony. In return, the administration would oversee the provisioning of essential supplies, infrastructure, and maintain order.

CHAPTER SIX

The JAMC Katanu

R aynor gasped for air and winced at the pain in his stomach. The room was dark and smelled of stale air and dust. He probed the wound gingerly with his fingers. It was still wet, still bleeding. He wondered how much blood he had lost; how much time he had left.

He felt through the pouches in his utility belt, discovering his Link was gone. He listened for any signs of activity, but there was only silence from within the enemy ship. He remembered the man in the robes and the mutant who had stabbed him. There would have been others, but where were they?

His wrist-light awoke when he pressed it, casting an eerie white glow around the workshop. He looked around, trying to locate some medical supplies: a panel on the wall marked with the universal blue circled wings. He tried to stand but pain forced him back to the floor. He reached out and dragged himself along the ground. Sharp pain raged through his body with each movement. Blood seeped out from the hole in his stomach, smearing across the ground as he dragged himself towards salvation.

A half-empty case of med-discs was his reward. He rummaged through the sleeves and found a green one, which he placed next to his wound to ease the pain. It melded into his skin and he sighed at the immediate relief. He placed a tan-coloured patch over the wound which fused with his skin and stopped the bleeding.

He picked out a purple med-disc, looking closely at the white markings engraved on it. The discs were all long past expiry and no longer manufactured, so he wasn't surprised to find one here. It was essentially a narcotic, used to treat serious pain. He put it in his back pocket.

He searched around an equipment locker and found a retracting sword that used the same tech as the doors in *Galaxy*. The black grip fit nicely in his hand, and when he thumbed the switch on the side, the blade flicked into existence. He swung it around, getting a feel for the weight, and marvelled at the simplicity of using a bladed weapon in an age of smart-rounds and energy blasters. It made sense for outlaws to resort to this kind of tool with limited access to Colony-built weapons or the ability to maintain them.

Raynor wondered where *Galaxy* was, and if anyone had realised he was missing. He limped over to a makeshift terminal. It didn't look like the regular interfaces he was used to. This one was a rat's nest of cables and wiring, haphazardly held together by plastic strips and metal panels. He started tapping away at the interface and tried to bring up a connection with *Galaxy* but most of the systems were locked out.

He heard the muted clunks of metal latching followed by the low drone of a motor spinning down. Another ship, perhaps, or a transit pod. Two shadowy figures emerged from one of the airlock hatches, dragging a limp body between them. One was wearing Raynor's spacesuit and the other had loose-fitting grey robes imprinted with a symbol of the sun, often used by outlaws. The limp body between them was Jake. Raynor hobbled over to a suspension field grapple and lowered himself into the shadows to hide.

Robes spoke in a low growl. "Now we've got an extra passenger, what do we do with him?"

"Doesn't matter. Secure him in a storage locker and we can deal with it later," the man in the spacesuit said. He approached the terminal and Raynor heard the distinct chime of a connection request. "Gavryn, we're on board. Get us out of here."

"Did you get the Artifact?" Gavryn replied.

"We weren't leaving without it." Spacesuit lifted a small black box, and Raynor instantly recognised the exigent cargo.

The Artifact, they had called it.

"The light of the Divine shines on us," the voice said back. "Gavryn out."

Spacesuit turned to address Robes. "Forge, once you've finished securing the hostage, I need you to come over here and see if you can open this."

Raynor waited until both of them were focused on the container and then attempted to move slowly and cautiously across the workshop without making a sound. Twice he had to hide behind relic rock-crushing machines to let the pain ease. Robes—Forge—was hunched over the exigent cargo at a workstation. A data-node control cable snaked from the workstation to the container. Forge tapped at the interface, glanced at the container, tapped again. He was trying to hack his way in, but so far nothing seemed to be working.

Raynor held the purple med-disc and reached for the sword hilt on his belt and then reconsidered. There was a long metal tool that resembled a wrench on the floor nearby. Raynor picked it up and felt its weight. With all his strength, he flung it at Forge. The pain forgotten, he watched it spin through the air, almost as if it were in slow motion. He didn't wait for it to strike. Instead, he sprung into motion, emerged from the shadows, and caught Spacesuit with a right hook to the face. He turned back to ensure the spanner had hit its mark and saw Forge slumped over the workbench, a spray of blood coating the interface.

As Spacesuit hit the deck, Raynor moved in with the med-disc and placed it on the outlaw's neck. The narcotic would only require a few moments to hit his bloodstream.

Raynor looked up at Forge. Blood splattered the interface, head rested on the workstation. Raynor checked for signs of life, but the impact from the wrench had cracked the man's skull. He hadn't meant for it to be fatal, but it was done now. With a great deal of effort, Raynor managed to drag the body over to the storage locker where Forge had stowed Jake. Raynor didn't want Spacesuit to wake up and see what had happened, so he removed Jake, checked that the boy was still breathing, then hastily stuffed Forge inside and locked it again.

Raynor turned his attention back to Spacesuit; head swaying, eyes tracking something imaginary around the room.

Raynor spoke slowly and evenly. "I need to know what the endgame is here."

Spacesuit stared back blankly and blinked.

"Let's start with your name," Raynor suggested.

"Sssssssssirec." He drew the sound out like the hiss of a snake.

"So tell me, Sirec, where are you taking us?" Raynor tried to sound friendly; he made his tone of voice warm and inviting. " *Pywayrah*," he said, giving his hand an odd look.

"What is that? Is it a place?"

"You know... I saw that mutant kill you. Why aren't you dead?"

Raynor clicked his fingers. "I need you to focus. How many others are on board?"

Sirec grinned. "Just us and the pilot."

"How did you find out about the exigent cargo? Who sold us out?"

"Fuck you." Sirec giggled.

Raynor reached for his new sword and the blade extended out in front of him. He considered it for a moment, letting the silent threat hang in the air. "What is the Artifact?"

Sirec licked his lips. "It's the key."

Raynor hoped he hadn't drugged Sirec past the point of making any sense. He prodded him in the neck with the tip of the blade. He drew a drop of blood, but the outlaw seemed to be immune to the pain, thanks to the narcotic disc. "The key to what?"

"To the Baulkham Dynasty... to victory."

Sirec's voice trailed off and his head began to sway again. Raynor had no idea what the Baulkham Dynasty was. Probably what this group of outlaws call themselves. He studied his sword and the tinge of red running down the tip. One dead outlaw and one dead mutant. A thought tugged at him; kill or be killed. Sirec would have tossed him out an airlock for no reason other than being an inconvenience. All he had to do was thrust his blade into the outlaw's throat. He would be doing the Colonies a favour, after all. Ridding the system of one more outlaw. Raynor shook his head. His justification for killing the outlaw fleeting. He could simply take Jake and the exigent cargo and use whatever means he had to escape.

Something caught his eye when he turned away from Sirec. The rare element that the mutant was supposed to trade him. He returned to the mutant's body and recovered the containment capsule. He grabbed the exigent container—the Artifact—and went to the airlock. A short-range transit pod was still latched.

The ship rumbled and shook. Raynor darted over to the blood-splattered interface and accessed a live-feed from outside. The ship had landed in a large, empty hangar. But there were no stations out here. By the size and design of it, he figured they must be in an Avis-class cruiser. This was a Martin Space Combat Fleet ship, but the assortment of outlaws gathering outside said otherwise.

Sirec laid on the ground nearby, still wearing Raynor's spacesuit and it was still fitted with Persephone's blaster. Raynor hastily stripped it off the stoned outlaw, stood in the boots, and the suit closed around him. A damaged spacesuit and a blaster was better than nothing. He held his arm out straight in front of him and the suit's targeting system booted up in his ocular lens.

One of the large hangar doors groaned open and light flooded the compartment. Eight outlaws armed with outdated Martian combat armour and energy blasters ran up the ramp and took aim at him. A man wearing a Captain's uniform styled with a gold sash walked up to him and glanced over at Sirec still rolling around on the ground. He turned to Raynor. "Welcome aboard the liberated battleship *Pywayrah*."

DATAFILE

MSCF Pywayrah

NODE 1

The Martian Space Combat Fleet *Pywayrah* is an Avis-class Battleship commissioned in C1084.

NODE 2

The Avis-class Battleship was designed to be a fully independent unit which could be deployed for strategic response missions and long-range patrol. It carries a crew complement of 312 people which includes 200 combat marines plus operation and support crew.

Armaments include 4x Nightwatch ultra-heavy particle-beam cannons, 8x Eclipse rapid-fire plasma turrets, 16x point-defence cannons, 6x torpedo rails with the ability to deploy its entire complement of 600 long-range missiles in under a minute.

NODE 3

The ship disappeared in C1089 under suspicious circumstances. No distress signal was received, nor was any debris ever recovered.

CHAPTER SEVEN

Android

Lisa awoke to the dim light of emergency illumination strips. The artificial gravity was almost non-existent, and she was strapped to something so that she couldn't shift around unintentionally. Her internal chronometer told her she had been out for over an hour. She looked around and recognised the familiar layout of the infirmary. She could see Appel at a workstation. The ship hand looked up from her work, softly pushed herself into the air, and gracefully floated towards Lisa.

"How do you feel?"

Lisa's internal diagnostics told her that the damage had been repaired to an acceptable degree with ninety-eight percent efficiency. She felt her stomach and found that someone had dressed her in a new uniform. There were no longer any external signs of her wound.

"I gave you some med-discs to speed up the work your nanites were doing," Appel said. "I have to say, it's rather impressive what your body's capable of. I've never treated a cyborg before."

Lisa eased one of the straps and propped herself up on her elbows. "What happened to the power?"

"I don't know exactly. But those outlaws somehow managed to disable Red, shut down the reactor and lock us out of just about every system on the ship."

"'Just about'?"

"We have emergency life support and lights. That's it."

Lisa released the rest of the straps on the makeshift examination bench and pushed herself towards the entrance. Most of the internal doorways in the ship were made of semi-solid-state panels which blinked open when unpowered.

"Where are you going?" Appel asked.

"To see what I can do to help."

Lisa glided through the ship in microgravity. One quick push enough to take her the length of a corridor. She guessed Rob would be at the reactor, located in the centre of the engineering deck. It took less than a minute to navigate the darkened corridors to the now-open bulkhead to the engine rooms.

"Hello?"

She grabbed a handhold in the door frame to turn into the room and shrieked as she collided into a body, floating just inside. She recoiled in shock, then stared in confusion as it drifted away. The thing had no apparent signs of life. No pulse, minimal heat, sections of exposed circuitry; it looked like a robot wearing human skin. A monster in the darkness of the emergency lighting.

Androids were somewhat a relic of the past—with humans fearing any sort of technological replacement of their flesh and blood—replaced by purpose-built robots in all shapes and sizes, built with limited programming and non-threatening design.

"Hello," it said back to her. It sounded almost human.

"Are you…" Lisa let the words hang.

Its head tilted quizzically. "Alive? Well, yes… and no."

"More no than yes," a voice said from beyond the android.

Lisa drifted around the body into a spacious power plant with four large tubes, each one originating from a different direction and intersecting at a sphere, which was so big she was unable to see the top and bottom.

In the dim light, she could see a short, round, bearded man tinkering with a control board in an access hatch at the front of the sphere. She didn't need a datafile to tell her that it was Rob, the ship's engineer.

"You see," Rob continued, "Abel was once the technician on the ship. That was until he got caught up in the tectonic inverters during some routine maintenance and was turned inside out."

Lisa was horrified. "You mean to say that you've taken the mind-scan of a dead man and reanimated him with a robot body?"

"Exactly!"

"Why would you create such an… abomination?"

"Abomination?" Rob pushed himself away from the control board and drifted slowly towards Lisa. "That's a bit of a harsh assessment for someone who has more mechanical organs than organic ones. Philosophically speaking, you and he are like cousins."

Lisa crossed her arms. "Except that I'm still alive! My organs have been replaced or augmented, but I'm still a human being—"

"Are you now? I suppose those neural processors, or the synchronous Link or the enhanced sensory perception implants make no difference to how you think? How you act?"

"I still think," Abel said. "I think as though I am alive. I still have my memories, sometimes."

"But it's not real," Lisa said. "It's just the illusion of thought. You're no more alive than Red."

"So, what's the problem then?" Rob reached up and patted his creation on the back. "He isn't quite finished yet. He was in stasis until the power went down and I had to wake him up. I need to use his microreactor to jump-start the ship. Now, did you come to help or are you just here to get in the way?"

Lisa got to work helping Rob connect Abel's power source into the reaction chamber. Then, with the help of Diputs and Lazarus, they powered up the suspension field array, which contained the violent fusion reaction that powered the ship. It started as a tiny spark at the centre and then swelled like an eruption, burning plasma surged and flared like a raging maelstrom of fire. A miniature sun grew in the centre of the sphere—hotter and brighter than the one at the centre of the solar system—powerful enough to sustain an entire colony. The lights brightened with a hum as the systems powered up, and the sweet scent of fresh air filled her nostrils as the atmosphere began to cycle on full capacity.

She looked over at Abel, removing the now obsolete connections from his own power source. He was another example of how this ship, this crew, was pushing the morally questionable boundaries of human potential. In a strange way, it was almost like she even belonged here.

With the power restored and all systems operational, they moved to the control room to devise a plan of action.

Red showed her how the attacker and one other outlaw had docked with *Galaxy* using an older model transit pod, forcing their way in using Raynor's Link, and hacking Red's systems from the interface in the lobby. Red put up a decent fight, coming up with new counter processes to try and regain control, but it wasn't enough. Whoever the other outlaw was, they knew their way around complex digital environments.

As soon as long-range communications were back online, Lisa slipped away and requested a connection to Swift. Which, to her surprise, he accepted.

"You're late," he said. When she told him what had happened; that two of the crew were missing, one of them being Raynor, Swift laughed.

So? What should we do about it? she asked through her synchronous Link.

"Do nothing. I put you on that ship to keep an eye on them, not to get involved. Have you found anything that I can use to challenge their Nexus charter?"

Lisa was aghast. *There is an outlaw ship out there with two captive Martian colonists and an exigent cargo container. And you want me to do nothing?*

"Was I unclear? Need I remind you that *Galaxy* is a non-combat cargo ship with no weapons or battle experience? Have the crew resume their prearranged flight plan and I will send a Cluster out to the belt to investigate."

Lisa knew that the nearest cluster of Martian battleships would be at least half a rotation away. She ended the connection without any formalities.

When she returned to the control room, Diputs and Rob were at an interface. A red track glowed on the holo, heading outwards from the asteroid.

"What did you find?" she asked.

"We were unable to track their Links," Rob said. "But we've been able to follow the ship's unique drive signature here." He tapped on the blip at the end of the line and the display zoomed in on the target. "The ship we encountered was once a mining skip registered to the Jupiter Alliance. It's since docked with a much larger ship which Red identified as being an old Martian battleship."

Red sent her the datafile; the *MSCF Pywayrah*. Listed as missing ten cycles ago. There was no distress call, no wreckage or debris, no trail, nothing. It was like the ship had just stopped existing. The phenomenon was simply unheard of. And no one wanted to even question the fact that the entire crew might have gone rogue and defected to another colony, or worse, become outlaws.

It had only taken two hours to catch up with their target. Lisa's plan hinged on exploiting a weakness of the battleship's point-defence grid to get onboard. From there, she would need to access the computer system, locate the abducted crew and get the exigent cargo. All without being detected by the outlaws operating it. This was her first solo assignment. Two rotations in and she was already planning to disobey Swift's orders.

Rob accompanied her to the lobby where she donned a light atmosphere suit and climbed into the transit pod. He handed her a small spherical contraption. It was a chrome ball with engraved lines running around it and a single button sunk into the smooth surface.

"What is this?"

"Just something that may help you on your way out. I want you to give it to Raynor. He'll know what to do with it."

"What if... what if I don't find them?" *Alive*, she left out.

"I have every confidence that Raynor is still alive. I've seen him get out of worse situations."

Lisa raised an eyebrow. "Really? Like what?"

"Not important. If you can't find them, get the exigent cargo, destroy as much as you can and get to a transit pod."

Lisa checked her weapon charge as she boarded the pod.

"Timing is critical," said Rob. "If you're still aboard when you reach their defence perimeter—"

"I know. Hope your calculations are accurate."

Rob grinned. "You're the one with a cybernetically enhanced brain."

The pod door locked. The interface in front of her displayed the view outside; then the blackness of space with a curbing green line to track her path. There was a moment of silence, then the heavy clunk of the camlocks releasing. The sharp acceleration pressed her back as it boosted away from the ship like a missile. *Galaxy* was still moving at high speeds, compared to the battleship. The pod used its small energy thrusters to push it towards the outlaw battleship. She knew she would be coming in too fast. To their scanners, it would look like a weaponised projectile hurtling towards them.

She kept a close eye on the range indicator and just before the pod entered the ship's defence grid, she blew the emergency release on the hatch and launched herself out towards it.

The pod exploded behind her as the automated point defence cannons obliterated the impending threat. She would be identified only as a loose bit of debris flying off—no threat to the armoured hull plating.

The readout overlaid in her ocular lens showed her distance to the target. Five hundred metrons came up quickly. At four hundred she could see the barrels of the ship's PD cannons, and could see them tracking the debris. Three hundred. She fired the suit's micro-thrusters, tensed against the hard deceleration. Her ocular display highlighted the entry hatch. If she had still had regular organs, the pressure would have crushed her to death. But her body resisted, and she was able to reduce her velocity fast enough to mag-lock on to the hull without ripping her arms off.

She looked up, five metrons away from her target. These outlaws might have been smart, but they weren't thorough. The old access codes still worked on the pressure door and she slid inside without any objections.

And that was the easy part, she told herself.

DATAFILE

Daily Log of Robert Crane

C1098 S22 R9

Abel was just in an accident. We were trying to stabilize the core containment when a charge-regulator exploded. The suspension field gave out and he copped a full burst of radiation. Reen is treating him in the infirmary but the exposure to the core has literally destroyed the cells of his body. I don't think there is much we can do.

C1098 S22 R11

Reen has done all he can but it wasn't enough. Abel passed away at 1302.

C1098 S22 R14

Reen has kept Abel's brain in stasis and Red is helping me take a full scan, converting his mind into usable data. I haven't been able to find any reference to past research or development on this kind of technology, which is strange. Nexus regulations only apply to SmartSystems and genetic mutations. Abel doesn't fit under either of these categories.

C1098 S23 R24

Raynor arranged to get all the parts I need from a robotics lab on Lunar. I've had to custom-build many of the components. I still can't find any information on the Nexus regarding androids, which is why I think there is a great need to keep my work on this subject hidden.

C1098 S24 R2

I've run some initial tests and it seems large parts of his memory matrix won't load. It's as though they are all trying to surface at once. He is progressing well with motor control, though. We are having meaningful discussions, which demonstrates that the logic and reasoning pathways are working, but he hasn't mentioned the accident. I don't think he has grasped the full reality of the situation.

C1099 S1 R18

I am still calibrating the transfer nodes on the memory matrix. Abel is slowly starting to remember who he is. Soon he will remember his own death. Not looking forward to that conversation. I have decided to try and re-grow his skin from a DNA sample, but I still have to try and find a way of grafting it onto the machine and then keeping it alive. At the moment he looks like a robot skeleton wearing Abel's skin as a coat. I don't have any mirrors in here, so it's ok.

CHAPTER EIGHT

Scourge

Jake's eyes shot open, his head ached. He floated in a suspension field, familiar from his Habitat, but this one held his limbs firm, preventing anything but the slightest movement. He struggled against it, his muscles strained against the invisible force. He tried to call out for help but his voice was muffled. The last thing Jake remembered was being in the lobby on *Galaxy*, power failing, being forced into a pod at gunpoint. Then, blank.

The room looked the same as any infirmary he had ever been in; white-panel walls, grey floors, round platforms; suspension field emitters, marking twelve treatment bays. Each bay had its own set of controls and medical equipment which he knew nothing about. Raynor floated one of the bays. Red-faced, he thrashed against the field, sweat beading on his forehead, droplets hanging in zero-g. Jake was surprised to see him, glad that he was still alive.

A woman with short blond hair sat at a workstation nearby. She looked up from her work and, seeing that they were awake, picked up her Link and walked over to his bay.

"Hey," she said. "They're both awake now. Ready for questioning." Favouring him with a brief unsettling smile, she turned and left through an open door.

Across the room, he heard the hiss of a door sliding open. Two large men in grey robes strode into his field of view and carefully inspected their captives. One had green eyes and a dark beard speckled with grey hair. He gave Jake a warm smile, which would have been welcoming under normal circumstances.

"My name is Amis and this is my companion, Kellar. It's nice of you to join us. Though we would have preferred it if you hadn't murdered one of our brethren."

Raynor mumbled two syllables which, from the tone, sounded like they were intended to be offensive.

The bald one, Kellar, seemed to understand and grinned at the muted slight. "You are still alive by the grace of the Divine. You have a chance to atone for your actions and seek forgiveness."

"The black container that we took from your ship," Amis continued. "It contains something immensely valuable to us. But we have been unable to open it—"

"The container is made from a material we have never encountered before," Kellar interrupted. "Nothing we have is tough enough to break through it."

Amis spread his arms. "If you would be so kind as to help us open it, we will reward you with a quick death. Otherwise, we will be forced to kill you slowly; over and over and over again."

Both of them smiled as they nodded slowly to each other.

Amis adjusted a control on the interface. The hum of the emitters eased, but Raynor still floated in place. "Have something to say, do we?"

"Have you tried shoving it up your companion's ass?"

The outlaws chuckled.

"Slow and painful it is, then," Amis said. "After what you did to Forge, I was hoping it would come to this." He pushed the slide control all the way up and Raynor screamed. His eyes bulged and his veins protruded as his muscles strained against the surge of pressure. Jake tried to shout his objection, but all he could hear was muffled shouts.

"Are you ready to tell us how we open this box and get the Artifact?" Amis said condescendingly.

Raynor gasped for air. "Ask nicely, you stupid—"

Raynor was interrupted by another wave of pressure. He let out a blood-curdling scream as he was crushed by the immense force. This time, blood seeped out from his nose and formed crimson orbs in front of his face.

Amis looked at Kellar. "He doesn't think we're asking nicely. Can you think of a nicer way to ask this man for some assistance?"

"I think a little electro-therapy would be nice." Kellar said with a grin.

Amis placed two small circular plates on either side of Raynor's temples and then pressed the button on the control interface. Raynor convulsed and thrashed about, jolts of energy grounding to the emitters above and below. His muscles bulged and tensed, causing his body to bow as he seized. His eyes rolled up into the back of his head, muscles spasming and face contorting. Jake wanted to look away, but he couldn't. Raynor's defiance was beyond comprehension. Did he even know how to open it?

Finally, the electric shock stopped. Raynor went limp, gasped for air and then spat the blood from his mouth.

"How about now?" Amis said.

Raynor didn't say anything. Amis pushed the suspension field slider all the way up and hit the button. Raynor spasmed again, eyes in the back of his head. Blood was coming from his ears. His muscles strained and contracted so quickly it looked like he was going to be torn apart. Every second that passed by filled Jake with dread, until finally it stopped. Raynor floated in the suspension field, completely still. The biometric readout on the interface flashed red, a high-pitch tone prompting action. Amis pressed on the alert and the device pulsed briefly. Raynor gasped back to life. His eyes were wide and distant.

"And how about now?" Amis asked again, mockingly. He took a drawn-out swing and plunged his fist into Raynor's jaw. Raynor was so dazed that he didn't even raise his arms to try and block it. The impact knocked him out of the suspension field, and gravity dragged him to the floor.

Jake thrashed against his suspension field again, still shouting muffled objections. Anything to buy Raynor just a little more time. Kellar released the pressure to Jake's suspension field and kicked him to the floor as well. Jake's head rang as his head hit the ground and the room spun.

"Speak!" Kellar demanded.

Jake coughed and panted to regain his breath. "He doesn't know how to get into it!"

"Do you really expect us to believe that?" Amis said.

"If he knew, he would have told you. He's trying to keep you focused on him to protect me."

"Protect you? Why?"

"What does it matter? Neither of us know anything. All of this is a waste of time."

"Thing is," Kellar said, "nothing we are doing is able to open that box. So one of you is going to tell us, then we will let you die. Maybe neither of you knows how to open it. If that's the case, you might want to figure it out before your friend's brain turns to mush and we get started on you."

"Just wait! Let me try." Jake didn't consider himself to be brave. But he had an idea. And at the very least he could allow Raynor to recover a bit.

Amis and Kellar exchanged a glance.

"Try what?" Kellar asked curiously.

"All cargo storage containers are encrypted with a security protocol which uses our Links to verify access. Give me my Link back and I should be able to open it."

"We don't need him," Amis said. "We could just hack his Link."

Kellar folded his arms. "How? They killed Forge, remember? No one else has half the skill he did with Colony tech."

Amis scratched his beard. "Ok, we will take you to it, but don't try anything heroic."

"Or we'll cut your hands off," Kellar added with an amused grin.

Kellar pulled Jake to his feet and gave him a shove towards the exit. Jake looked back at Raynor who was still on the floor, barely breathing. There was fresh blood on the floor pooling around his stomach.

Amis knelt down, pulled out a med-disc from his pocket, and placed it on Raynor's neck. "This is a little something the biochemical techs call 'Rage'. Consider it a gift from Sirec."

"It's going to be a wild ride." Kellar laughed.

They walked through several corridors, then went down five levels in a mag lift. Jake tried to commit to memory how they got there. They entered a large ornately decorated shrine room. Tapestries lined the walls in a circle, surrounding a large cabinet in the centre. The Artifact box sat inside the cabinet upon a small fabric square that cushioned it. The cabinet was engraved with strange carvings and patterns, most of which Jake didn't recognise. The one he did recognise though was the symbol of the sun in the centre, its rays reaching out. It looked like what a child would draw if you asked them to quickly sketch the sun, but to these people, it seemed to have some far greater significance.

Amis shoved Jakes Link at him. "Now, get to it."

Jake picked up the box and looked at it intently. It was engraved with strange symbols and designs he had never seen before. There were no buttons, catches or pressure switches, nothing to indicate that the box was meant to be opened. On one face, there was a picture of a snake eating its own tail with the words etched around it that read;

I AM THE BEGINNING OF THE END, AND THE END OF TIME AND SPACE. I AM ESSENTIAL TO CREATION AND I SURROUND EVERY PLACE.

Jake held his Link up to scan the container. His Link presented him with an actions menu and he tapped the lock icon. It asked him for an encryption key, which he didn't have. There was a sequence he could enter which would discreetly activate a distress signal, so he placed his thumb and two fingers on the Link's surface and made three counter clockwise motions, then a confirmation message asked him if he was sure he wanted to proceed. He selected yes, and the message disappeared, returning him to the encryption key input.

"Do you know how to open it or not?" Kellar said impatiently.

"This is a riddle," Jake said. "An old one. The answer is 'E'. Perhaps it means the key *is* 'exigent'." He keyed it in while the outlaws watched intently. When the words INVALID KEY flashed across his Link, Amis snatched the box and placed it back on the shrine.

"Come on!" Kellar said, smacking Jake across the back of his head. "I knew this was a waste of time."

Jake slid his Link into his pocket and kept his head down. "I'm sorry. I thought it was worth a try."

Amis pushed him out into the corridor. "We'll find out if your friend truly knows. Let's see if he feels more talkative after he watched you bleed out."

The ship was much larger than *Galaxy*. Each corridor and junction looked identical. By the time they had returned to the torture room, they had made eight turns as well as the trip on the lift. He was pretty sure they had returned a different way than they had taken to get there.

Raynor was back in the suspension field being treated by the blonde woman, which Jake thought was peculiar, given their intentions.

"What are you doing, Dia?" Amis said. "He doesn't deserve your mercy after what he did."

Dia looked back at him defiantly. "If I don't treat him, you won't be able to continue your interrogation for much longer." Something in her voice told Jake that it wasn't the real reason.

The lighting dimmed, pulsed a bright red, and a siren began to sound throughout the ship.

"What's that?" Kellar said.

The alert siren sounded twice and then a general announcement was broadcast from every interface and echoed throughout the corridors. "We are under attack from the Martians. All hands to report to assigned duty-stations and prepare for ship-to-ship combat."

"Quick, we'd better find out what's going on." Amis hit Jake with his weapon.

The force of the blow caused Jake to fall to the floor. He felt a sharp pain, followed by a rush of adrenaline. The door closed on his view of the fleeing outlaws. The illumination strip framing it changed to red.

Jake pushed himself up and rubbed his head. "Well that was fast," he said cheerily.

Raynor looked over at him. "What are you so happy about?"

"Didn't you hear that?" Jake asked. "I bet it's *Goliath* on the way to rescue us! I sent them a message to come help!"

"You did what?" Dia asked.

Raynor groaned. "It's not on the way to rescue us, you idiot. It's on the way to destroy *Pywayrah*. Our deaths will be just collateral damage."

Jake looked at Dia, acutely aware that she hadn't yet made a move to restrain him. He put one hand on the ground and slowly pushed himself up. Dia moved closer to the control interface and gripped a small medical implement at her waist like a weapon.

"I'm not going to hurt you," Jake said trying to sound calm and reassuring. "You heard what's happening. That ship is here for us. If you turn us over, then—"

Dia laughed bitterly. "You expect me to believe that your battleship will just let us go?"

Jake knew she was right, but he had little else to offer.

"We will continue to fight to the last," she said without conviction. "We will not give in."

"Maybe *they* will. But *you* don't have to." Jake took one step closer with his hands out cautiously in front of him. "You don't strike me as a killer. You don't have to be one now." Another step. "If you let us go, no one has to know. We might not even get all that far. But you get to go out with integrity, knowing that you are not a murderer."

Jake could see the dilemma in her eyes as she held her ground, now within striking distance. He reached out to the interface. She watched without making a single move. He slowly released the suspension field and Raynor floated to the floor next to her.

Raynor stumbled, then lunged forward and wrapped an arm around Dia's neck in a sudden movement, getting her in a headlock.

"Raynor, wait!" Jake yelled.

Dia dropped the implement and grabbed at Raynor's arm. He whipped her around and they both collapsed on the floor. Raynor held tight.

"You know, you might not be a killer," Raynor said in a strained voice, "but you're still one of them."

There was a rage in Raynor's eyes that scared Jake. It was like he had lost some part of his sanity when they had tortured him. That sort of abuse had to take a toll on the mind. And the body.

Dia managed to elbow Raynor in the ribs. He released his hold and writhed in agony on the ground. He didn't make any attempt to get up, so Jake grabbed him by the arm and slowly helped him to his feet.

Dia had already composed herself and went over to the door. The locks cycled and she stood aside.

"Why?" Raynor groaned.

Dia said defiantly, "I am one of them but I'm not like them." She looked out the door and then back at him. "They will do a better job of killing you then I ever could."

For some reason, the way she said it, Jake didn't believe she meant those words.

Raynor braced himself on one of the workbenches, reached for his utility belt and clipped it around his waist. He opened a pouch and gripped an unfamiliar device, which extended into a long silver blade. Dia took another step back.

Jake raised his hands. "Raynor, I really don't think you're in any state to—"

"Don't try and follow us," Raynor uttered.

Jake gave Dia an apologetic look, then followed Raynor out of the infirmary. The corridors were a panic of people running in all directions. Flashing emergency lights, noise and shouting assaulted the senses.

Raynor could barely walk, but he leaned in towards a passing outlaw and thrust the sword into him. The outlaw's eyes went wide in surprise, he fell backwards and Raynor followed him to the ground. Another tried to pull Raynor off him, but Raynor used the momentum to slash back, severing his arm. Raynor regained his feet and indiscriminately swung the blade like a drunk, left and right, trying to hit anyone within reach. Further down the corridor blasters hissed, and Raynor dropped to the ground amongst the bodies. Jake took cover around a bend and looked back to see three outlaws charging towards them.

"Raynor!" Jake yelled over the noise.

Raynor didn't respond. He unholstered one of the dead outlaw's sidearms and fired back.

"Shit," Jake exclaimed. "We need to get out of here!"

Raynor's eyes were wild with rage and his face was covered by blood. He kept shooting until there was no one firing back. The alarms continued to ring throughout the corridors and the lights flashed.

"Where is the exigent cargo?" Raynor huffed. "Can you get back there?"

Jake nodded and began leading the way to the shrine room. He hoped that they didn't encounter anyone else on the way. While he understood the immediate need for violence, Raynor's utter contempt for life troubled him. Raynor had been nice to him since he had been on *Galaxy*, but now he realised something else; the man was extremely dangerous.

DATAFILE

Gravity Drive

NODE 1

A Gravity Drive is a reactionless drive which can generate a focused artificial gravity well in front of the ship, and the ship 'falls' forwards at speeds relative to the gravity well's power level.

NODE 2

Since the G-drive creates an artificial gravity field around the ship, its speed is not limited by mass, but rather, by energy. The more energy the ship can safely generate, the stronger the gravity field in front of the ship and thus, the faster the ship can accelerate/decelerate.

Suspension fields are typically used internally in conjunction with the ship's drive to mitigate dangerous g forces from being exerted on the crew and maintain a comfortable 0.38 g environment.

CHAPTER NINE

Infiltration

Lisa's spacesuit was lightweight and offered no protection from weapon fire. It was certainly no substitute for her mech-armour, which would have come in handy right about now. If she hadn't returned it to the armoury on *Goliath*, she would have been able to tear through this ship like it was made of plastic. She would have been unstoppable. Instead, she had only her cybernetic enhancements and a small energy-blaster strapped to her thigh. It meant she had to be careful not to raise the alarm.

She opened the seams and pulled her gloves loose. They hung at her wrists, leaving her hands free to use the nearby interface. Each junction in the corridors had one, so she walked up to the panel directly in front of her, placed her hand on the surface and closed her eyes.

The physical contact wasn't entirely necessary, but it meant she could bypass any authentication sub-routines that might have given her away.

Navigating through the ship's systems was a breeze compared to the restrictions that Red had imposed, preventing access to most of the systems on *Galaxy*. This ship had disappeared before the Cyborg War, so it was not designed to resist her abilities, even suppressed as they were.

The security grid gave her eyes on Raynor and Jake. They were in an infirmary, floating in suspension fields. She flicked through feed after feed, but found no sign of the stolen cargo. The logs also came up empty, so she started looking through the crew manifest. The original captain, Tyrance Reuben, was still in charge. He was alone in his chamber three decks up.

She took the service tunnels, a labyrinth of crawlspaces running through the walls and between decks. If it weren't for the navigation overlay from her ocular implants, she would've had no idea where she was going. When she reached the command deck, she pushed on the hatch and it clicked open. She looked around. Nobody was in there, so she emerged into the corridor.

The crew complement was over three hundred when the ship had disappeared. Now the count was at one hundred and fifteen, according to the recent logs. She wondered if there had been many objectors when the captain went rogue from the Colonies. She imagined their frozen corpses floating around in the vastness of space in the outer ring.

Lisa reached the entrance to the captain's suite, took a deep breath and gathered her thoughts. Once the door opened, she would have to act fast to ensure she kept the advantage.

She drew her blaster and the charge reading appeared in the corner of her vision. The security override admitted her to the dim chamber. Her eyes adjusted quickly and Lisa assessed the room. Inactive interfaces lined the mostly empty space, with one wall harbouring fold-away compartments for living utilities:

sustenance, sleep, sanitary, and storage. Tyrance sat on a plush cushion in the centre of the room with his legs crossed and eyes closed. She was on him before the door was fully open, leapt into the air and kicked. His head whipped back with a snapping sound as her foot connected with his face.

She hoped she hadn't killed him.

Lisa grabbed the Captain by the neck and took aim at his face. She felt his pulse. Still alive.

"Where is the stolen cargo?" she said. The muscles in his neck tensed and his expression hardened. She pressed her knee harder into his chest. "Where is the stolen cargo?

Tyrance choked out a laugh. "What are you going to do? Kill me and then take it back? All by yourself?"

"That's right, Captain Reuben. And if you don't tell me where it is, I'll simply kill you and question the next person I find."

"You'll have to do better than that! There are over one hundred of us onboard. Each and every one of us would gladly die for this cause."

"What could possibly be so valuable that you would give up your lives to retrieve it?"

He scrunched his eyebrows. "You would kill for it without hesitation, and you don't even know what it is!"

"Then enlighten me," she said through clenched teeth.

Tyrance smiled defiantly and slowly shook his head. She forced him to his knees, put her gun to his neck. She hesitated.

The room shuddered. Her first thought was that they had hit something, or rather, something had hit them. The lights flickered and Tyrance whipped his arm up knocking the gun away from his head.

She fired. The energy charge seared the ground next to his head. He grabbed her shoulders, bracing her as he brought his head up to meet hers.

The impact from their heads colliding was like a shock grenade. Lisa blinked away the static and by the time the ringing in her ears had subsided, she had been slammed on her back and Tyrance was on top of her, a knee at her throat. The muzzle of her own blaster pressed into her skull.

His Link buzzed and a small, distorted voice from it said, "Captain, it's the Martian capital ship and three destroyers. ETA is six minutes. One missile made it through the point defence from the first volley. That was just a warning, sir. They won't miss once they're up close. Do we stay and fight or turn and run?"

"Friends of yours, are they?" Tyrance said, dragging her up off the floor.

"You can't outrun them," Lisa said defiantly.

"That's right." Tyrance pushed her to one of the wall-interfaces. "That's why you're going to talk to them."

With his free hand, he brought up the comms menu and made a connection to the control centre. "Prepare for battle. Get the artifact off the ship and give the enemy everything we got." Then he set it to open broadcast. "My name is Tyrance Reuben, captain of this liberated battleship. I have three of your people and an extremely rare Artifact on board—"

Swift appeared on the interface. From the command deck on *Goliath,* he looked like a king sitting on his throne. The cam tracked his face, zoomed-in. "Mister Reuben. You and your crew are charged with appropriation, abduction, dereliction of duty, attacking a Martian transport, and the assault of one of my officers. I order you to power down your weapons and surrender for processing. You will release all prisoners unharmed and secure the cargo for repossession."

"I don't think so," Tyrance said forcefully. "Here's my counter-offer. You let us go and I'll drop your people in a pod before we get to the Kuiper belt. We keep the cargo and you never have to see us again. No one needs to get killed."

"You really think I'm going to let you get away with a Martian battleship and the stolen cargo for the sake of three lives? There is no negotiation here. If you refuse to comply then I'm left with no other option than to destroy our stolen property."

"You're bluffing," Tyrance uttered.

"He really isn't," she said through gritted teeth. "Stopping a threat is more important."

Tyrance pressed the blaster harder into the side of her face and Lisa turned her head slowly to look at him. His jaw was clenched, and his forehead was slick with sweat. He pulled the trigger, but nothing happened. The blaster clicked with each try.

Lisa spoke loud enough for Swift to hear. "You know I'm the only one who can fire that weapon, right?"

Tyrance's eyes went wide and Lisa swung a fist at him.

CHAPTER TEN

The Artifact

Jake stood silently looking at the small black container as it sat in its shrine. So much stress all caused by this one little box. He almost didn't want to recover whatever was inside. They should just get out of here whilst they still had the chance. But he didn't think it would be wise to challenge Raynor in his current state, half-mad from the drugs and torture.

Raynor collapsed on the floor at the base of the shrine, picked up the container, and turned it over in his hands, inspecting it from all angles. Jake couldn't tell if the blood on Raynor's hands and clothes was old, fresh, or from one of the outlaws he had cut down. He pointed at the riddle. "'I am the beginning of the end, and the end of time and space, I am essential to creation, and I surround every place.' What do you think it means?"

Raynor ran his bloody fingers through his hair. "It's a riddle. Perhaps a password?"

"I know. The answer is 'E'. Already tried that. Right after I sent that distress—"

"Wait, do you have your Link still?"

"Well sure. I pocketed it while the outlaws were busy berating me for wasting their time."

Raynor grinned. "Give it to me."

Jake handed him the Link, then watched Raynor log-in to access a different set of tools to what Jake was used to seeing. "What are you doing, exactly?"

"The riddle isn't the answer, it's a clue. That design on top is an ancient symbol called Ouroboros, which means 'eternal'."

"So *that's* the encryption key?"

"Not quite. Eternal is an encryption algorithm which Rob gave me to… acquire something for him. It's suspiciously related to how we ended up in this situation in the first place."

Jake raised an eyebrow.

Raynor turned back to the lines of code flittering across the Link. "Never mind."

The encryption key input went green and an eye-looking symbol appeared briefly before fading to black.

The lines on the box lit up, suffusing the room in a golden aura. Tiny gears in the sides—which Jake thought were just part of the design—began to turn and the box made a buzzing sound as it vibrated. Raynor held it in both hands and waited. Jake took a step backwards.

With a click, the box cracked open. Four corners retracted outwards to reveal its precious contents. A small triangular golden shard glimmered in the light. Lines engraved into one surface formed a pattern and disappeared into a jagged edge, which suggested it had been broken off from something larger.

Raynor hesitantly reached in and picked up the object. He tilted his head back, closed his eyes, stretched his shoulders, and inhaled deeply. When he opened his eyes again and looked at

Jake, he looked… happy. Like a heavy burden had been lifted from him. It all happened the moment he touched the shard.

"What is it?" Jake whispered.

"I'm not really sure," Raynor admitted. "But I feel incredible. The outlaws were calling it, 'the Artifact.' Apart from that they never really said what it was—"

"Or what it's for," Jake added.

"No."

"But whatever it is, it is obviously incredibly valuable for them to go through all this!" Jake said.

They stood looking at the golden shard for several moments. The only sound was the ringing alarms throughout the ship, the deep rumble of explosions, distant commotion of people dying, and turrets being fired. Raynor closed his hand around the shard and slid it into his pocket.

An explosion that felt and sounded closer than the others thundered through the hull, causing them to stumble as the lights flickered.

"Whatever it is, it can wait. We need to get out of here," Raynor said. "I saw a wall of pods on the way here. Hopefully they're still working."

They ran through the corridors, the alarms flashing, and the ship rumbling with weapons fire. Jake's mind was running so fast, he could barely follow his own train of thought. They rounded a bend and ran towards a bank of transit pods. There was only one empty pod on the end, the rest appeared to have been launched already.

"Last one!" Jake said.

"Yeah, lucky us," Raynor agreed.

"Lucky us, indeed." The voice came from behind them. Jake spun around and saw the outlaw who had abducted him, weapon drawn and aimed at Raynor's head.

"You again," Raynor groaned.

"Yes, me again. And you are going to step aside and allow me into that pod."

"Damn," Raynor said slowly. "Sirec, right? I should have killed you when I had the chance."

"I was thinking the exact same thing. And by the will of the Divine, I'm still alive. Thing is, I'm not going to make the same mistake as you. If you get in my way, I'm going to kill you."

Raynor looked confused. "You going to talk us to death?"

Without hesitation, Sirec fired at Raynor. The discharge of energy cracked through the air and pierced Raynor's chest. The force knocked him to the ground.

Jake didn't think, he just acted. He surged forward. Sirec had no time to bring his weapon about. The outlaw fired again as Jake crashed into him. The bolt shot off to the side and burnt a large hole in the interior wall of the battleship.

Jake and the outlaw wrestled for control of the blaster. Two more shots discharged aimlessly. Sirec let go of the weapon with one hand and took a swing at Jake. He fell backwards but managed to keep his grip on the blaster, pulling Sirec down on top of him. The look in Sirec's eyes was pure rage. Then changed to agony. Jake looked down to see a shiny steel blade protruding from the outlaw's ribs.

Raynor yanked back the blade and stumbled. Jake pushed Sirec away and looked up, astonished that Raynor was still standing. He had just taken the full brunt of a high-powered energy weapon, and apart from the scorch mark on his chest, he appeared almost completely unharmed.

"Secure his weapon," Raynor snapped. Jake picked up the blaster, looked at it in his hands, and took a deep breath.

"You'll never get away from here alive." Sirec coughed, blood spraying over his robes. "You get into that pod and you will be shot down."

Raynor flicked his hand and the sword's blade retracted into the hilt with a snap. Sirec's breathing grew short and erratic. "You know what? You're right, maybe you should go first." He grabbed Sirec's robes and tossed him into the pod. "Have fun out there."

He pressed a button on the interface next to the pod and the door snapped shut. The ejection sequence thunked and the pod shot out from the wall, leaving only a door-sized portal in its place.

"What is wrong with you?" Jake said.

Raynor shrugged in response. "What?"

Jake had hoped Raynor's exposure to the Artifact, and the serenity it seemed to give him, would have quelled his violent anger. "You had already incapacitated him! Now you've given him our only means of escape."

"You worry too much," Raynor said. "You think that's the only pod on the ship?"

Jake shook his head. He looked out the viewing portal at the pod, still powering away from them, almost too small to track. Blue lines streaked across its path, and the pod turned into a large ball of light, then quickly faded.

"They just shot the pod!" Jake yelled.

"You can thank me later," Raynor said. He stopped at the nearest interface and waved his hand across it. "No point getting in a transit pod if it's just going to get shot down. We need a lift from *Galaxy*."

Jake looked around nervously, hoping that no one else would sneak up on them.

"Oh shit," Raynor said. "Have a look at this." Jake approached the interface. Raynor was trying to access the comms, but there was a flashing red code on the screen.

"What is it?"

"It's the distress code from the *Arcanna*, a ship I used to serve on. The cyborg is trying to get my attention." He brought up two images, side by side. One was the Supreme Commander and the other showed Lisa next to an outlaw who had a blaster pointed at the side of her head. Raynor kept tapping away while the conversation played out.

"...no one needs to get killed," the outlaw said.

Bit late for that, Jake thought.

"You really think I'm going to let you get away with a Martian battleship and the stolen cargo for the sake of three lives?" Swift said with an amused half-smile. "There is no negotiation here. If you refuse to comply then I'm left with no other option than to destroy our stolen property."

"He's bluffing, right?" Jake asked nervously.

Raynor let out an unimpressed sigh. "Nope."

"How can Swift just leave us for dead?"

"It's not that simple," Raynor said. "Swift has an obligation to suppress the outlaw threat to the Colonies."

"What about his obligation to us!"

Lisa said something while he was talking. The outlaw was wide-eyed, Lisa threw a punch at him. The outlaw ducked and the blaster was gone.

Swift looked away and the connection terminated.

"Look!" Jake yelled. "We have to get up there and help her!"

"Why would we help her? She was sent to incriminate us."

Because it's the right thing to do? "Maybe she was, but who sent her *here*?"

Raynor hesitated at that.

Jake kept pressing. "She risked her life to come here and help us."

"You don't know that. She could just be here for this." Raynor held up the shiny golden Artifact.

"So what if she did? She would have still needed a plan of escape."

Raynor narrowed his eyes. "All right. Let's go get the cyborg."

CHAPTER ELEVEN

Escape

Raynor ran through the ship. He touched his shoulder, and his fingers came away red with blood, but it didn't hurt. Despite his injuries, despite torture, he felt strong, ready for anything. He wondered what else the Artifact was doing to him.

Every now and then the ship would shudder, taking another hit from the space battle outside. He didn't let it slow him. Now that Raynor had a rudimentary idea of where he was going, every so often he had to stop and consult the deck plans to ensure they were still on track.

Jake ran behind, gasping and panting. "How do you know where we need to go?" he asked through ragged breaths.

"The captain's suite is always on the ops deck close to the control room," Raynor said. "That's where we'll find them."

"What makes you so sure they would be there?"

"That's where the communication originated from." Raynor paused at an intersection. "Now, would you shut up and let me concentrate?"

They moved through the winding maze of corridors, the explosions became more violent. It was a sure sign that they were nearing the operations deck where Swift's forces would be concentrating their fire.

Outlaws who had obviously abandoned their posts—or were escaping from damaged parts of the ship—ran past them without even giving them a second glance. Raynor's rage had subsided since his fight with Sirec. It was actually something about the way that Jake had looked at him, a mixture of fear and disappointment, which had caused him to reflect on his behaviour. Drug-induced or not. A flush of shame washed over him for giving in to his animal instincts—and perhaps his combat training—to destroy the enemy. If they were all going to die anyway, did it even matter?

When they finally reached operations, a quick review gave him the exact location of the captain's suite. He stopped to one side of the door and prepared to enter, sword in hand. To his surprise, Jake took up a similar position across from him, stolen blaster at the ready.

The ship was at battle protocols, overriding all door locks. Raynor opened the door and stepped in just before Jake. Lisa was inside, facing off against the ship's Captain, Tyrance. Blood stained his uniform, flowing from a flattened nose. The snarl of his chain-sword was loud in the confines of the cabin.

Lisa was breathing quickly. Both of them stopped to look at him for a moment before the captain decided to chance another swing at the cyborg. She was too quick and dodged out of the way.

Without even thinking, Raynor charged at the outlaw and screamed as he swung his blade. The captain deflected the blow, sending sparks flittering through the air. Raynor took two more swings, forcing Tyrance backwards.

The crack of blaster fire snapped past his head and the interface panels behind Tyrance shattered in a flash of sparks and flying debris. Jake's aim was atrocious. Almost in response, the ship jolted violently, and air started hissing out of fresh breaches in the battleship's hull. The lights flashed orange as the area lost containment and the ship was unable to hold in the atmosphere.

Lisa raced towards the entrance and slapped her hand against the interface. It flashed red—the door unyielding. Raynor turned his attention back to Tyrance, just in time to see him slide into a hidden access duct.

"It's no good," she yelled over the hissing. "The corridor has also lost containment."

Raynor grabbed Jake by his jacket and pulled him across the room to the escapeway. "Through here," he yelled. There was no interface or trigger that he could see to open it. Lisa had caught up, and without a word, placed her hand against the panel and closed her eyes. The cover-panel slid away, fresh air rushed out from the darkness.

The passage was only wide enough for one person at a time, so he let Lisa and Jake go ahead of him. Once he was inside, the door snapped closed, plunging them into relative silence and total darkness. Raynor pressed on the wrist-light contained within the fabric of his clothing. Lisa and Jake had done the same, illuminating the narrow passage.

"What do we do now?" Jake asked.

"We can't stay in here," Lisa said. "Tyrance will likely try and find reinforcements."

"You know, we had this under control," Raynor said. "We didn't need you to come and rescue us."

"Oh didn't you now?" Lisa laughed. "This is what you call under control? Who says I came here for you anyway?"

"Hey, we just saved your ass back there—"

"Uhhh, so are we getting out of here?" Jake interrupted.

Lisa glanced back accusingly. "There are several exits; the control centre, storage locker, conference room—"

"That one," Raynor said. "Tyrance would've either gone for the locker or the control centre. We don't need to follow him into a trap."

They shuffled along to the end of the narrow corridor and Lisa worked her skills on the door once again. It opened onto a room with a long table and a row of viewports along the far wall looking out into the starry void.

They spilled into the room and just as Raynor crossed the threshold, movement caught his eye. He hurled himself back behind cover as the ear-popping sound of a sonic disruptor crashed into them. The shock wave swept Lisa and Jake off their feet and tossed them across the room. Raynor was still standing. He only had a brief window where the disruptor would be recharging, so he leapt forward, sword in hand. The captain dropped the disruptor and reached for the chain-sword slung over his back.

Raynor charged. Raising his sword above his head, he put his full force into the downward swing. Tyrance blocked—the spinning blades of the chain-sword caught on Raynor's blade, sending blue and white bolts dancing indiscriminately around them. Raynor whipped the sword around and struck again and again. Tyrance held his ground, swung back with a force that nearly threw Raynor off balance. Raynor blocked another strike, went down on one knee, and released all the force by sidestepping out of the blade's path. Tyrance almost lost his balance but managed to regain his footing. Now, Tyrance had his back to Lisa, who was on the floor recovering from the sonic shockwave. She managed to pull herself to Jake's fallen blaster. It hummed back to full-charge, she took aim. The sharp cracking sound filled the room. Three times fired, and Tyrance fell back, writhing in pain. Raynor went for the throat and the blade passed clean through it. Lisa covered her mouth, then quickly composed herself. Raynor realised he was covered in blood and most of it wasn't his.

Before he had a chance to ask what her escape plan was, the ship groaned and shuddered. After being tossed into the air there was no longer any artificial gravity to bring them back down so instead, they were flung into the wall. Lisa landed gracefully and kicked off the wall to glide over to him.

"Here," she said, holding out a metal sphere that looked like a bionic eye. "Rob said you'd know what to do with it."

He stared, nonplussed. "What's this? What am I..." His eyes narrowed, a memory stirring. "We might just survive this after all." He took the device and inspected it closely. The room was already starting to fill with thick smoke masking the dim emergency lighting. He could just make out the single round button and a

groove that ran around the length of the device. He pressed the bu
tton.

Nothing happened.

He tried twisting it either side of the groove and the device cracked open. Then he remembered. Raynor reached into one of the pouches on his utility belt and pulled out the glowing blue cylinder. He shattered it against the wall. *Fuck, I hope this doesn't give me some kind of radiation poisoning.* Raynor plucked out the rare element from the floating debris and held his breath.

He realised that both Jake and Lisa were floating near him, watching intently, eyes fixed on what was in his hands. He placed the element carefully in the device and sealed it back up again. He exhaled, his thumb slid over the button.

"Wait!" Jake said. "What is this thing meant to do exactly?"

"If I remember correctly, it's supposed to turn us into light and transport us wherever we want to go in the blink of an eye."

"That's impossible," Lisa said.

"Only one way to find out," Raynor responded. "Besides, it's either this or suffocation."

"Okay," Lisa agreed. "Let's do it."

"Should we be holding hands?" Jake asked.

Raynor thought about it for a second. "Couldn't hurt." He wished he had been paying more attention to Rob's explanation. Jake and Lisa had already locked wrists, so Raynor grabbed hold of Lisa with his free hand, took one last deep breath and pressed the button.

The light engulfed them. It was like they had just exploded into whiteness. All of the noise and smoke and the ship melted away. Time felt like it was frozen.

He couldn't see anything, but he was aware of where he was, who he was. Instinctively he held onto that knowledge of himself, protected it. He became aware of Lisa and Jake. He knew them almost as he knew himself. But they seemed to be blowing away, like leaves scattering in the wind. He gathered them up and held onto them.

He could feel Jake's anxiety. There were memories buried deep down that he didn't want anyone to find. He had come to *Galaxy* for a fresh start.

But there was also fear. Fear of him. Raynor saw himself through Jake's mind, ruthlessly taking lives like they meant nothing.

Raynor withdrew from the thought, and curiosity attracted him to Lisa. She was so confused, trying to make sense of what was happening that she just let him slip by her attention. Her thoughts were far more erratic. He saw flashes of Swift. A memory of a thousand voices, crushing her. The deaths. So many deaths. She screamed at him to get out.

What was this?

What had they become?

Were they dead?

Was this the afterlife that the outlaws believed in?

Rob's voice echoed in his head. *You're pure light-energy. You can travel back to the ship.*

How do I do that? But the voice apparition didn't respond.

He expanded his awareness. Out past the crippled battleship, past the Martian ships, past the inanimate rocks in the asteroid belt, and focused on *Galaxy*. The distance seemed insurmountable, but between thoughts, they were simply there. Then he was aware of Diputs shielding his eyes.

The transition back to his normal body felt like striking the ground from a great height. Everything hurt, but nothing in particular was causing him pain. He opened his eyes and his stomach lurched with a sense of vertigo.

The three of them collapsed on the ground in a heap.

"What the fuck just happened," Lisa said, the terror clear in her expression.

"I think I'm going to be sick," Jake groaned, still lying flat on his back.

Raynor pushed himself up to his feet, testing and feeling all the different sensations like it was the first time in his own body. "I'm going to go and find Rob, if anyone needs me."

DATAFILE

The Star

NODE 1

The Star is a quantum state transference with a conduit of antimatter resonance. It is powered by a rare element known as Krontonium which exists in a state of concurrent light-matter. Its origins and whereabouts remain unknown.

CHAPTER TWELVE

Debriefing

Lisa still couldn't quite comprehend what had happened. One moment they were on the outlaw ship and the next they were on Galaxy.

Appel had checked her over in the infirmary with a cold professionalism that implied the ship hand was still holding a grudge over the treatment of Reen. After being cleared, Lisa returned to her Habitat to run her own system diagnostics. There were no abnormalities except for a point-zero-three-second blackspot when she had travelled with Raynor and Jake using the Star device. She spent the remainder of her time resting and putting together her report for Swift. There was still so much she didn't understand. So much she couldn't explain.

Lisa emerged from her Habitat for a tube of Organix. She found Raynor leaning against the wall. He looked at her through narrowed eyes and she felt that the tension hadn't eased even after surviving a life-threatening ordeal together. Raynor leaned against the wall next to the Organix dispenser, twisted the seal off his tube and took a generous sip of the fluorescent green liquid inside. She felt like she had intimately known him for the briefest of moments, but the details had flitted away like air in the void.

"You reported back to Swift yet?" he asked casually.

Lisa selected a tube. "No, why?"

Raynor shrugged. "Seems like you'd want to go over it all with him before the debriefing."

Lisa was irritated more than surprised. It made perfect sense that they would have to answer for the exigent cargo. But she'd expected to have been informed about any briefing from Swift directly.

"Thanks for your help," Lisa said, "with the outlaws, I mean."

Raynor looked thoughtful for a moment. He let the silence drag. "Right place, right time, I suppose."

Lisa nodded. "I wanted to ask you... about that device."

"The Star?"

"How was that even possible? I've never experienced anything like that."

"No one has. At least not in over a million cycles, according to Rob."

"How does Rob know so much about it? Where did he get it from?"

"Truth is I don't really know. Every time I ask he changes the subject."

Lisa narrowed her eyes. "How am I even going to explain this to Swift?"

"Don't. I'm just going to say we escaped in a transit pod."

"I can't, I—"

Raynor leaned in closer to her. "If you want to find out more, maybe you should stick around a bit longer. It's up to you."

It was the middle of the rotation when they landed on Mars. Lisa took a pod with Raynor and Diputs to the transit station at the edge of Genai. The crescent-shaped colony sat on a flat plain between sharp, rocky mountains and a glistening blue ocean. The city itself reached up into the sky, with shaded glass buildings growing incrementally in size towards the middle. It reminded her of an extravagant crystal tiara.

A transway carriage took them through an underground network of tubes into the Nexus Administration building. They were ushered into a bland meeting room filled with a grey oval table with ten seats distributed evenly around it. The far wall was predominantly a window which gave them a view of the sprawling city.

Lisa took a seat near the entrance. Diputs seated himself across from her. They remained in companionable silence while Raynor stood looking out the window. From the height of the surrounding towers, Lisa estimated that they were about halfway up the building.

The sliding door hissed open again and Swift strode into the room. By instinct, Lisa rose to greet him, but he walked right past her and claimed a position at the head of the table. He was followed by a man with bright orange hair by the name of Cliff, from the Mars Logistics Entity, who nodded a greeting at Raynor and Diputs before taking a seat halfway between them and Swift. Then, a representative from the Mars High Council, Carl Larkell—a grey-haired paternal figure with reassuring eyes—took position one place away from Swift.

The last to arrive was the Nexus Arbitrator, Eumon Saan. His black hair and dark eyes added to the severity of his scowl and made him look like a man who wasn't impressed to be having this meeting. Saan looked around the room, and Diputs, who had kicked his feet up onto the chair next to him, sat up straight under the focus of the Arbitrator. Once they were all seated, Saan brought up a holographic info-display on the interface in front of him.

Lisa glanced around the room and noticed that Raynor seemed to be staring at Saan, focused on a small silver pin on his collar. She zoomed in on the metal disc to get a closer look at the triangle and circle design etched into it, wondering if it held some significance for Raynor.

"The reason I've called this meeting," Saan began, "is to go over the events relating to the loss of an item of exigent importance."

"What about Reen?" Raynor interrupted. "When are you going to tell us what's happened to him?"

Saan scowled. "As far as I'm aware the incident is still under investigation and is none of my concern." He inhaled sharply. "I've reviewed all of your accounts from the recent events; your ship had reactor troubles, you set down on an asteroid to make repairs and were set upon by outlaws who abducted two crew members and appropriated the exigent cargo. One of the crew sent out a distress call, which Swift responded to. Lisa disobeyed a direct order not to get involved and managed to recover the crew but not the cargo and the enemy threat was neutralised. Did I miss anything?"

Lisa shook her head. She was impressed that he had managed to say all that in almost a single breath.

"Yeah," Raynor said, "you missed the part where we almost got killed for that 'exigent' cargo. What I'd like to know is, what was so important about it and how did those outlaws know that we'd have it? *Galaxy* is near untraceable, there is no way they came across it by accident."

Saan gave an amused grin. "It means that there's corruption in the Mars Colony. Likely in the MLE." Lisa glanced at Cliff, who was biting his fingernails.

Councillor Larkell tapped his fingers on the conference table. "There's no use in speculating. Where's the proof?"

"That's what I intend to find out," Saan agreed. "I'm authorising a full investigation into the MLE and *Galaxy*. The ship will be grounded and searched, the crew will report for disciplinary coaching."

Diputs slammed his palms on the table. "This is ridiculous! We don't need 'coaching'."

Saan glared at him. "Be glad that I'm not revoking your Nexus charter."

Swift laughed. "You can't seriously be allowing them to continue flying around without any oversight."

"I don't see why not," Larkell said. "They will be grounded for the duration of the full investigation. The infirmary tech, Reen, has been detained, thanks to your efforts. What further risk do they present?"

"We'll see." Swift narrowed his eyes.

"As for the exigent cargo," Saan said impatiently. "A search of the wreckage has been inconclusive. It's possible that in the confusion of battle, the outlaws managed to escape with it."

Larkell stood. "Thank you for your time, Arbitrator. The rest of you are dismissed."

"Au revoir," Cliff said; a farewell from an ancient dead language that dull people used to sound sophisticated. The others filtered out as well without so much as a goodbye. All except Swift. Lisa remained in her seat and waited patiently for him to address her.

Once they were alone, Swift said, "Want to tell me what's really going on?"

"Whatever do you mean?"

"You know exactly what I mean. You had every opportunity to expose Raynor as a liar and an insurgent but instead, you defended him!"

"I was just doing my job—"

"Were you? Or are you making this about us?"

"*I'm* making this about us?" Lisa said, trying to keep her voice even. "Why did you really put me on *Galaxy*?"

"I told you it's a need-to-know basis."

Lisa clenched her fists. "'Need to know?' How do you expect me to be of any use if I don't know what's going on?"

Swift placed his Link on the table. It started emitting a faint static noise. He took a deep breath and lowered his voice. "Something insidious is going on in the Nexus and I suspect this crew is somehow involved. I wanted to put pressure on them to see how they'd react."

Lisa leaned back and crossed her arms. "So did you get what you wanted?"

"For now, I think it would be best for you to return to *Goliath*."

"No," she protested. "There is still more that I can do on *Galaxy*."

Swift leaned forward in interest. "Oh really? Do tell."

Lisa smiled. "How about this. I'll tell you when you need to know."

DATAFILE

Communication Log

-Ryan Swift to Lisa Separa-

C1099 S04 R09

My Dearest Lisa,

I'm currently sitting in a Nexus council meeting with a bunch of boring old fools arguing about resource allocation or whatever. I'm looking forward to being back on my ship... with you. I miss the thrill of battle. Fighting side by side with you against our enemies. I thought being the Supreme Commander would give me more opportunity to fight for Mars. Instead, it's all meetings and engagements where I'm expected to tell war stories to impress High-Value dignitaries.

I've been thinking about what you said, and I must insist that you reconsider my proposal for Unity. I don't care what people say about us. About you... If it means that I would have to give up my position, then so be it. They can demote me to Squad-Comm for all I care and send me to patrol the outer rim.

I know that if we formed a Unity, it would be challenging for both of us. But no good things come without hardship, and I feel like it would be better than the alternative. Things can't just stay the same forever. We need to grow and move forward.

I love you. See you soon.

-End Message-

CHAPTER THIRTEEN

Plunder

Raynor floated in the suspension field and tried to push down the growing anxiety which came from the memories of being on the outlaw ship. He had to remind himself that this was different. He was home. He was safe.

Appel worked on an interface next to him, intently focused on the technical readouts from the bioscans. She pushed a strand of auburn hair out of her face and tucked it behind her ear.

She seemed to be taking the loss of her friend and mentor—and all their research—fairly well.

"I really don't think this is necessary. I feel fine," he said.

"That's what worries me. Jake told me what happened. He said they tortured you, and their physician had to bring you back to life so that they could keep going. You shouldn't feel fine."

"But?"

"But all of the scans show that you are fine. In fact, better than fine. It's almost like you've slipped into an entirely new body."

"Maybe it was Rob's Star device? It did turn us all into light, after all."

"I don't think so. Jake's results were completely normal."

"Well then, I don't know what to tell you. Maybe the scanner's broken."

Appel gave him an impatient look, but he thought it was best not to tell her about the Artifact. Especially while they still didn't really know who sold us out. But he highly suspected that this strange device, whatever it was, had accelerated recovery and evoked the sense of euphoria he felt just from holding it.

In truth, he didn't really want to let go of it, but it would be essential to let Rob take a closer look in order to find out what exactly they were dealing with and where it could have come from. He had even kept it on him during the briefing while he lied to his superiors about how it was destroyed.

Appel dismissed him, having done all of her tests and scans, so he retrieved his utility belt and Jacket and headed out to meet up with Rob and Diputs. He knew exactly where he would find them at a time like this.

The infirmary opened into the lobby, which was only separated from the common room by an archway of hydroponic plants. Jake was there, checking over the plants by pointing his Link at them.

"Good work there, Jake," Raynor said. "Those plants wouldn't stand a chance without you."

Jake looked at him blankly. He slid his Link into his pocket and walked towards Raynor.

"Hey, uhhh, about what happened on the outlaw—"

"Don't mention it," Raynor said. "No, seriously. You know what you need? A drink. Come with me."

He didn't wait for Jake to respond. He made his way over to the mag-lift and Jake stepped in behind him. He selected the engineering level and the lift hummed into motion.

"Why are we going to engineering for a drink?"

Raynor shook his head as the doors vanished and he stepped out into the corridors. The only way to Rob's hideaway was via an isolated service tunnel that could only be accessed from an equipment storage locker. It didn't even show up in the ship's floor plan. It made getting out after a few drinks interesting.

Rob's voice was audible when they entered the service tunnel.

"—so then she says, 'what would embolden you to create this abomination?' and I said, 'This coming from someone with less biological material than the Organix dispenser'."

Diputs' laughter indicated he had already been there for a little while.

Raynor released a latch and the bulkhead door slid smoothly open.

"Woah." Jake looked around in wonder.

Raynor didn't normally reflect on how out of context the place was. The room featured a long black bar with five metal stools on one side, even though only the three of them ever occupied it and Rob always stood on the other side. He stood in front of the glass contraption with vertical tubes that made and dispensed dark golden alcohol.

The opposite wall, which Raynor normally had his back to, was filled by a large interface with technical readouts and live video feeds from around the ship. It really was Rob's unofficial control room.

The laughter stopped at the sight of Jake, replaced by a silent acceptance that Raynor had brought him here intentionally. Rob produced two small glasses and filled them from a bottle of the golden nectar.

"What is this stuff?" Jake leaned in and took a sniff. "It smells vile. Isn't this against colony regulations?'

Raynor grinned. "What gives you the impression we give a shit about colony regs?" He raised the glass to his lips and tilted his head back to let the warm burn of the alcohol flow down his throat.

Jake sat on the stool and took a cautious sip. He grimaced, then nodded as if he was appreciating it.

"So," Rob queried, "how was the briefing?"

"And what happened with the outlaws?" Diputs added. "You haven't said much since you've been back."

Raynor looked around at them. He had already told Rob as much as he needed to whilst returning the Star. "It was shit." Raynor pushed his glass towards Rob and the engineer instinctively refilled it. "But I managed to hold on to this…" Raynor took the Artifact out of his pocket and it clanked on the bar.

They leaned in closer to get a better look at the small triangular shard.

"What is it?" Diputs asked first.

"This is what was inside the exigent container. The one we were meant to deliver to *Altos-4*. This is what all the fuss was about."

Rob narrowed his eyes. "What's so special about it?"

"That's something I'm hoping you can tell me. You're the expert on ancient tech. It gives off some sort of aura. When I first got it,

I thought I was about to expire. But then I started feeling better, stronger, faster. I felt like a fog had been lifted from my thoughts. Despite the injuries I sustained at the hands of those outlaws, Appel told me I'm in perfect health."

Jake was nodding in agreement, while Rob and Diputs listened intently.

"Whatever this thing is," Raynor continued, "it's pretty powerful. And a lot of important people seem to be interested in it. Which is why Jake and I both left it out of our reports. As far as our superiors know, it was destroyed along with the *Pywayrah*."

"You do realise that if Lisa finds out—" Diputs started.

"Then let's make sure she never finds out."

"Okay," Rob said. "But it's on you if she does. What do you suggest we do with it?"

Raynor picked it up again and relished in the relief that washed over him. "I'm going to hold onto it for now. I want you to run some scans on it though, see what's inside. It seems impossibly small for something so powerful."

Rob grinned. "It's obviously just a fragment of something larger, too. I wonder if this could lead us to more Artifacts."

He tucked it away, stowing it safely in his pocket. "I have a friend on Lunar who owes me a favour from that off-the-record retrieval we did a little while ago. He might be able to provide some insights about where it came from."

Raynor turned his attention back to his drink and they sat for a little while in companionable silence.

"Hey, one more thing, while I remember. Have any of you heard of something called the Baulkham Dynasty?"

Diputs choked on his drink but said nothing. Raynor filed that bit of information away for later.

Rob shook his head. "No, sorry. Why do you ask?"

"Whoever they are, they might just be behind all of this."

CHAPTER FOURTEEN

Reparation

The hover platform zipped across the long dark warehouse. Cliff hung onto the handrail, the wind whipping through his orange hair. The platform began to slow as he neared his destination. He used his Link to activate the overhead lighting.

In truth, he didn't exactly know what he was looking for. He had been sent an anonymous tip that something unbelievably valuable awaited him.

Thousands of storage containers of various sizes and styles were stacked across the warehouse floor, stretching out for ten kiltrons in every direction. This complex was filled to the brim with valuable resources which the Colony needed to survive. This was but one of many similar warehouses. Though he reflected that Mars had long since passed the stage of being a colony in the literal sense, it was a vast civilisation covering the surface of the largest habitable planet in the solar system and expanded into space with a network of space stations.

His Link buzzed in his hand. Cliff read the writing that flashed across it.

UNKNOWN CONNECTION

A sense of dread washed over him. He took a deep breath and then hit accept. A mutant's face appeared. It was elongated and warped, with rough blue skin and spiky tufts of hair. Cliff recognised Ziak from their last conversation to negotiate the exchange of some genetic research for a rare element. It had taken Cliff subcycles of sifting through encrypted channels and following nefarious leads to track down someone who could retrieve what Rob was after. The risk was always high, dealing with mutants. If the Nexus had found out, he would have his Value annulled. But if the trade was successful, his reward would have changed everything.

Ziak's voice cut through Cliff. "What is the meaning of your betrayal?"

"Look, it wasn't my fault, okay?" Cliff shouted back.

"You sold us out to outlaws," Ziak snarled.

"No! That wasn't me. Someone much higher than I put something on the cargo ship which the outlaws wanted..."

The mutant leaned in closer. "Who?"

"I don't know, but they covered their tracks incredibly well. Hacked into secure nodes and erased everything, I heard."

"You lie convincingly to your own kind. Why should I trust you now?"

"They almost killed my people as well. What would I have to gain from that?"

"You primates have never been averse to sacrificing your own. We should be your masters. We *will* be once you have compensated us for our losses."

"You're forgetting our deal. You got what you wanted—"

"What we want, is to be recognised as the superior race, to be feared and regarded by your kind, not be hunted down and killed like animals." Ziak bared his razor-sharp teeth. "There is something else we need from you. Something big."

"Look, I think you may be overestimating my influence here. If you're going to keep changing the terms of our agreement, then I'm not going to comply with any more demands."

"And yet here you are. Complying. Who do you think sent you those coordinates?" The mutant grinned. "This is your last chance."

The mutant broke the connection. Cliff stared at the blank display of his Link. He had probably gone too far to back out now. Something was in that container; something they wanted. One last job, that was it.

Cliff arrived at his destination. It was a large crate, big enough to walk inside. He entered a code into his Link and the door opened for him. He stepped off the hover platform, footsteps echoing in the cavernous warehouse. The inside of the container lit up as he entered. He looked around, curiosity fuelling his courage. It held only a clear cylinder held by a bulkhead at each end with a tangle of tubes escaping from them. He walked over to peer into the cylinder, took a deep breath and rubbed the frost away from the outside. He took a step back.

Reen was frozen inside.

BOOK TWO

ANAMNESIS

Every cycle, leaders of the four Colonies gather to reflect on history's shortcomings. But when the Nexus uses the Anamnesis to announce the formation of a new space fleet, some see it as an opportunity to seize power for themselves. Malicious sabotage sends the Matias 1 Space Station hurtling towards the Lunar surface, threatening the lives of billions. Unlikely allies must put aside their differences and work together to prevent catastrophic destruction.

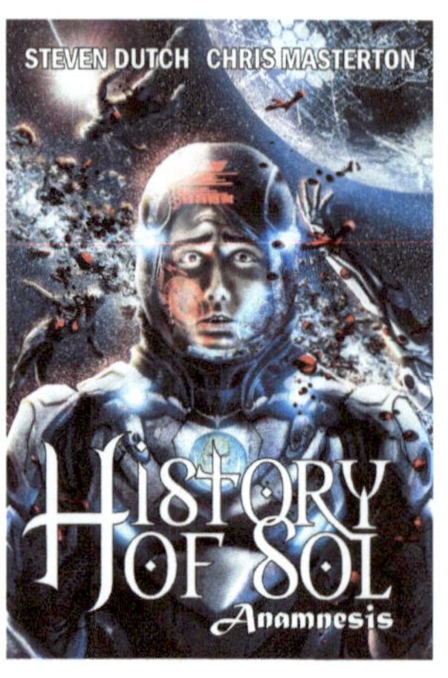

About The Author

Chris Masterton

Chris is a space nerd, tech enthusiast, and sci-fi author. He enjoys exploring themes such as the future of humanity, artificial intelligence, and the impact technology has on society. Chris has a background in software and graphic design.

Connect with Chris:

- www.chrism.au

- goodreads.com/chrismasterton

About The Author

Steven Dutch

Steven Dutch was born in Auckland, New Zealand but grew up in Sydney, Australia. He would consider himself a foodie, and enjoys most cultures' foods. He works a day job as a Cyber Security Service Delivery Manager and enjoys everything scientific and technological, which bleeds over into his writing often. He has always been fascinated by science fiction and magic, thinking there is a fine line between the two and enjoys writing stories meshing and melding the two together. He has been writing for over 12 years and has completed several writing seminars and courses.

Connect with Steven:

- goodreads.com/stevendutch

History of Sol

History of Sol is an action/adventure sci-fi novella series set in the distant future.

Find out about the latest releases and where you can meet the authors using our social media links:

- historyofsol.com

- facebook.com/history.of.sol

- instagram.com/historyofsol

- twitter.com/historyofsol

Glossary

- **Enforcers:** Responsible for maintaining law and order

- **Foreseer:** Manages and assigns roles based on the needs of their Colony

- **Observer:** Spy/Intelligence gatherer

- **Peacekeeper:** The highest level of Nexus administration

- **Datafile:** An automated file system that gathers and sorts all information in the Nexus

- **Data Crystal:** A small quartz disk that serves as a mobile data storage device

- **Habitat:** A self-contained living area on smaller spacecraft

- **Interface:** Computer

- **Krontonium:** A rare element used to power the Star

- **Link:** Communication device / Mobile personal interface

- **Mitron:** Microscopic unit of measurement

- **Millitrons:** Tiny unit of measurement

- **Centron:** Small unit of measurement

- **Metron:** Medium unit of measurement

- **Kiltron:** Large unit of measurement

- **Nexus:**

- **a) name -** The governing body uniting all of the colonies under the 'Nexus Treaty'

- **b) technology -** A colony-wide shared communication and data system

- **Node:** A subsystem component of a Nexus or Datafile

- **Organix:** Liquid sustenance

- **Outlaw:** A general term used to denote people without Value

- **Robotoid:** A small self-mobilised robot

- **Rotation:** The time it takes for Mars to complete one rotation around its axis

- **Sub-Cycle:** 1/24th of a Cycle

- **Cycle:** The orbital period of Mars to pass once around Sol

- **Tectanium:** A super-strong metal derived from Titanium and enhanced with nano-tech

- **The Artifact:** A small shard of unknown material and origin

- **The Star:** A quantum state transference with a conduit of antimatter resonance (converts matter into light for brief periods of time)

- **The Terranean Expanse:** An asteroid belt between Lunar and Venus

- **Theridium Alpha:** A rare form of radioactive material found in the Kuiper belt

- **Unity:** A formal partnership between two or more people

- **Value:** Economic recognition based on contribution to a colony